Chico Boy

GINA HOOTEN POPP

Copyright © 2016 Gina Hooten Popp

ISBN: 0-9979558-0-5
ISBN-13: 978-0-9979558-0-4

This book is dedicated to those who need to squish their negative thoughts.

CONTENTS

ACKNOWLEDGMENTS

My gratitude goes to my family and friends for their support during my writing journey.

CHAPTER 1

The day could have gone either way for Chico Boy. Maybe it was the fact his pogo stick was working so well that made it lean toward being a good one. After all, how could you not feel good when riding on a pogo?

"Get off that damn pogo stick and come with me." The voice belonged to Talula, his best friend since the third grade.

"Don't curse, Talula. It ain't attractive on a girl."

"Don't say 'ain't.' It makes you sound less smart than you are."

Chico Boy continued to pogo and the result were his words were timed to his bounces." I cain't . . . *boing* . . . quit . . . *boing* . . . saying 'ain't' . . . *boing, boing* . . . oh, no . . . oh." And just like that, he pogoed headfirst into a parked car. It was a brand new 1974 Catalina Station Wagon, but he reasoned it only made a tiny mark, nothing worth tracking down the owner over. He, on the other hand, had quite a big dent right on his upper forehead near his hairline.

"Let me see, Chichi." He knew Chichi was her pet

name for him when she was trying to be extra nice. And that meant he might be hurt bad.

Sitting down on a nearby curb, he waited patiently as she used her dirty fingers to part his hair. He felt her digging around in his wound as she simultaneously pushed on a bump that had formed underneath the fresh cut. Talula was a tomboy through and through. He tried not to wince in front of her because she would notice and comment.

"Is it bleeding?"

"A bit. We'll wash it later. Right now, we need to go feed Silver for Mr. Jamison."

Chico Boy shook off the pain and handed over his pogo stick to Talula so she could put it across her handlebars like she always did when they rode together. Then he got on the back of her bike's long banana seat and settled in.

"Be sure to hold your legs up and out," she said as she took off. Luckily, they didn't have far to go in their small East Texas town since she didn't have the strength to go fast with him on board.

As they bumped along on the old bike, Chico Boy said, "Last night I dreamed I was riding a motorcycle up a meat mountain."

"Raw meat? Or cooked?"

"What's the difference?"

"One's bloody, and the other isn't," Talula huffed as she spoke. Chico Boy could tell she was getting tired.

"It was raw—blood everywhere."

They quit talking—the only sound was of Talula's heavy breathing. When they got to the little shed where Mr. Jamison kept Silver's feed, she stopped and Chico Boy got off first. He looked around at the small wooden shed with its attached covered carport on the east side.

Mr. Jamison had originally built it for the trailer next door, but it ended up making a perfect shelter and storage place for his horse. When Jamison leased the place out a few months ago, he made it clear to the renters they would not have access to Silver's carport and storage shed.

The horse saw them coming and ran across the field to greet them. It was a beautiful sight to see him in full gallop with a red dust cloud flying close behind. Chico Boy knew Silver wasn't truly a white horse—he was only light gray—but Silver was as close to being true white as any horse he'd seen.

As Silver approached, Chico Boy reached out to stroke his nose. The day was hot and dry. Not even the birds were moving. The only sound came from people arguing in the nearby trailer.

"No . . . Sam . . . don't do that," were the only words Chico Boy could make out clearly.

Looking behind him, he saw Talula coming out of the shed carefully carrying the special feed Mr. Jamison had bought for Silver in a large bucket. The arguing next door escalated to a fevered pitch as Talula poured the feed into a big plastic tray. Now the words were easy to hear.

"No," a male voice trembled with fear. "Oh, my God. No."

"Sam, no," another male voice shouted.

Silently, Talula and Chico Boy watched Silver eat as they tried to ignore the fight next door.

Then . . . *Pop. Pop.* Two shots rang out.

In the silence that followed, Chico Boy ducked for cover behind the metal water trough. Talula froze. Silver started to neigh loudly, backing off from his food tray. Without even thinking, Chico Boy got to his feet and grabbed Talula's arm. He pulled her into the small feed shed and pushed her under one of the handmade wooden workbenches. He pulled a few boxes and boards in front of her. Then he went down to the end to the workbench and crawled under it. Little slivers of light came in from the half opened door. He saw the overturned bucket Talula had managed to carry back in with her.

Wiggling around, he sidled up to Talula, who was very still. He could see her eyes looking around wildly. She seemed to be having a little trouble breathing. He hoped her asthma wasn't acting up.

A door slammed on the trailer next door. Two sets of heavy footsteps were headed toward the feed shed. Silver neighed loudly and snorted. The footsteps moved around to the area where Talula had left her bike.

"Hey, a pogo stick," a gruff male voice said.

"And a bike," a deep, melodious voice commented in a worried tone. "Those two kids we saw earlier are still here."

More footsteps, followed by silence.

Next, a single set of footsteps moved toward the shed door. Chico Boy felt the thud of his heart in his head. A nearby dust bunny moved as the door opened wide. A large body darkened the doorway as it stepped inside and looked around. Chico Boy couldn't see the man's face from his position under the workbench and Talula had her eyes shut tight.

A second man entered the dark shed's interior. Chico Boy memorized their shoes as they moved a few sacks of the special feed and some loose rope around. The man with the gruff voice wore exotic snakeskin cowboy boots and the other dress shoes with tassels. Both pairs of shoes were expensive and both were covered with red dust.

"They're not here. Probably off at that creek over

yonder." The one in the cowboy boots was doing the talking.

"Still that's close enough to have heard."

The two men left the shed and moved out into the open. When they closed the door behind them, the small room immediately became stifling. Chico Boy shifted a bit and noticed Talula still had her eyes clamped shut.

Outside, Silver snorted and neighed. The two men tried to reassure the horse but their efforts were futile. After some muffled conversation, the footsteps retreated toward the trailer. In a few minutes Chico Boy heard the sound of a car engine engaging and driving off. He wondered where it had been parked since he hadn't seen a car anywhere around the trailer. It must have been on the opposite side.

Seconds later, he put his hands down flat on the dirty cement floor and started pulling himself out from under the hiding place. A nail scraped his back and he flattened himself out and pulled again. Soon enough he was standing upright.

Opening the door a crack, he looked down under the worktable. Talula was completely hidden by the boxes and boards. Moving a few, he found her with her eyes still closed. He was surprised she was so frightened because she was pretty brave for a girl. But she was only twelve years old. Every once in a while, the two years he had on her in age seemed like a lot more. Especially when she was scared like right now. Which wasn't often.

"Talula."

She opened one eye in response.

"Talula, we need to move. Get up."

Without a word, she slipped her tiny form out from under the table and went outside. The sunlight made them both squint. Talula's bike was exactly where she had left it. The pogo stick, however, was missing. Chico Boy did a quick search in vain. He knew the men had taken it.

"Talula, get on the bike," Chico Boy said gently as he held it out to her. "I'm going to run beside you."

Talula took the bike by the handlebars, her face stone. "We need to go back the long way."

"Why?"

"Because their car took off that way." As she spoke, the normal take-control Talula started to return. "And we don't even know if they were both in the car. I don't want to pass by in front of the trailer."

"Yeah, you're right." Chico Boy couldn't help but admire her quick thinking. Pointing to some nearby trees, he said, "Let's keep to the woods instead of the road. I'll push the bike."

Talula looked around. "Where's your pogo stick?"

"The murderers took it."

"Chico Boy don't say that! It could've been firecrackers." When he didn't answer, she continued. "I really don't think someone was killed. Not while we were just standing here feeding a horse." Her voice seemed to plead with him to tell her life was not that way, that bad things don't happen on ordinary days to average people going about their daily business.

He looked down at the sincere expression on her innocent face and took her bike by its handle bars.

"I'll push it through the woods," he repeated.

They walked along saying nothing with the cumbersome bike between them. It had been rough pushing it through the thick undergrowth in the woods in the places where they didn't have a clear path to follow. His ankles had taken a beating from the pedals hitting them, but he didn't dare take the bike out on the open road. He didn't want anyone following them.

As they neared his house in the older part of town, he glanced at his watch. It had taken them well over an hour to make it back going the long way.

"The shower feels good on my hurt head." Talula could barely hear Chico Boy through the thin bathroom door.

"Hey, did you notice I put out a towel and jeans for you on the back of the toilet?" She yelled to make sure he heard her over the steady stream of running water.

"Talula, did you come in here while I was in the shower?" he yelled back.

"No, don't freak out. I put them in before you got in the shower," she yelled back through the flimsy door, "while you were feeding your sister's cat."

Talula had insisted he wash the wound on his head. However, she was feeling a little strange because his mom, who was supposed to be home, was working double shifts at the restaurant and his sister was out with her friends. Now they were the only two there besides the cat and, as if the situation wasn't weird enough, she found herself yelling, "I couldn't find any underwear."

"That's because I don't have any."

"Not even for special occasions, like Easter?" She heard the water stop.

"Hey, come help me doctor my head wound."

Talula waited a full two minutes before carefully opening the door and poking her head around. She was happy to see he had on clothes. Well, not his shirt. Moving slowly inside the tiny bathroom, she noticed his muscles glistened on his still damp body as he shook his wet hair like a dog. Talula picked up a towel and dried off her arm where the droplets had landed.

Trying not to be obvious, she watched as he toweled

off his hair and looked at his face in the mirror. He was starting to get a little bit of a mustache, but it was blond and hard to see. Apparently, he was very pleased with the new growth because he kept rubbing his finger across it. Then she realized he was watching her watch him in the mirror, so she said in a very formal, doctor-like voice, "I'll need some antibiotic ointment."

She observed him open the medicine cabinet and dig around a lot of junk before pulling out a half-used medicine tube.

"Sit here." She nervously pointed to the closed toilet seat.

As she applied a dab of the ointment to his head, she gently held his hair back. Checking his head over for other cuts and bruises, she was very aware he was staring straight up at her. It made her jerk in surprise when he suddenly announced, "Did you notice how big my arm muscles are getting?"

"Yes," she said quickly before changing the subject as he flexed his muscles for her. In a very serious tone, she said, "Stop that. And let me see your pupils."

In an exaggerated effort, he opened his eyes extremely wide. She ignored his silliness. Putting her hands on either side of his head, she moved him toward the direction of the overhead light and stared directly at his pupils.

"Why are you looking at my eyes, Doctor? The bump is on my forehead."

"If one pupil is larger than the other," she said, "you might have a concussion."

"It doesn't matter if I have a concussion because we can't afford a doctor visit."

Talula continued her careful assessment. "Looks like your eyes are normal."

Just then, Chico Boy reached up and touched the side of her face. She held up her arm to stop him. As she tried to twist away he started tickling her stomach.

"Stop it! You're going to make me wet myself," she cried as she ran from the bathroom.

"Then why are you running from the bathroom?" He said as he pursued her down the hall, threatening to continue his tickle torture.

"Stop it! I mean it!" she said as she swatted at him.

Suddenly, she got very quiet. A pang of worry stabbed at her heart.

Chico knew it was time to knock it off.

"Are you okay?" he said. "Did I hurt you?"

She watched as his expression turned to concern.

"The shooting . . . someone got hurt today. And here we are goofing around."

"Would it make you feel better if I go back and look in the trailer?"

"I'll go with you."

"No, I'll do it after my tutoring class at the church. I'll take Big Mike with me. If we find a dead person, we can tell the cops what we heard and saw this afternoon."

"What if the person isn't dead? What if they're lying there hurt?"

"I'll go after class." He put an arm around her and hugged her close as he said it. She nearly hyperventilated. Sometimes she didn't think he understood the effect he had on her nerves. She liked him so much and he just seemed to think of her as one of the guys.

Snapping back to reality, she heard him say, "It needs to be dark."

She shook her head in agreement. He gave her a sympathetic smile, then he abruptly rubbed the hair on her head really hard in a twisting motion using the extended knuckle on his curled up second finger. A move he and Big Mike called a "nuggie." Talula's heart fell when she realized he was just being his big-brother-silly-sort-of-self. Obviously, he still thought of her as a kid. Lost in her thoughts, she watched absentmindedly as he went back to the bathroom to comb his wet hair in the mirror.

"Earth to Talula. Come in, Talula," he said in his best NASA astronaut communications director impersonation. "What are you thinking about so hard?"

"I don't know," she said as she followed him down the hall into his room.

Pretending to admire his trophy collection, she averted her eyes as he put on his shirt.

Without turning her head, she cut her eyes back to him. Once she was certain he wasn't looking at her, she turned around in time to see him open the top drawer of his desk. Rummaging to the bottom of a pile of papers, he pulled out a spiral notebook. The cover was pink—bright, bright, bright shocking pink. It even had a multi-colored butterfly sticker on the back.

She didn't know what to say, so she didn't say anything. But he did.

"This notebook's one my sister had leftover. I didn't want to ask Mom to buy a new one."

Gesturing at the flamboyant pink notebook, Talula asked, "How's the tutoring going?" She was incredibly proud of him for going to summer tutoring. She knew he was smart. He just hadn't gotten off to a good start this past year of school what with his parent's separation and his mom having to work all the time. There was no one at home to help him, no way for him to keep on track once he'd fallen behind.

"Actually, I'm surprised. I'm really making headway."

She heard a twinge of pride in his voice. "Wouldn't it be something if I could be somebody one day?"

"You're somebody. You're Chico Boy."

"Yeah, I could kill my grandfather for giving me that crazy nickname."

"I like it," Talula said as she tossed her hair.

"He named me Boy Boy. It's stupid."

"No, it shows you're half Mexican and half American."

"It's redundant."

"Wow, did you learn that word in summer tutoring?"

"I heard my substitute teacher, Miss Lancer, use it and asked her what it meant."

This Miss Lancer was really helping Chico Boy catch up with the class, you'd have to give her credit for that. The new substitute had even gotten him interested in current events. The other day, he had surprised her when he had made a comment about Nixon being subpoenaed to turn over the tapes. Talula was proud that he was going the extra mile to learn by watching the nightly news and reading the newspaper.

Leaning back against the wall with her arms crossed, she considered for the first time that he might not like his nickname. "Okay, Chico Boy," she said, "tell me what you want to be called and I'll start calling you that."

Without a second's hesitation, he shot back, "Allen."

Talula was shocked as she knew his real name was not Allen but Richard. "Hmmm, Allen's a nice solid name. But how about I tell everyone to call you Chichi like I sometimes do?"

"Chichi, I like it," he said.

"Then from here on out, you will officially be known as Chichi." She wrote the word *Chichi* on a page in his pink notebook and held it in the air. "So it is written, so it shall be done."

She noticed he laughed at her dramatic interpretation of Ramses from the recent movie about Moses. Her heart jumped wildly with delight as he lightly punched her shoulder before saying one more time, "Chichi—I like it. But wouldn't it be easier to just shorten my name to Chico since that's how everyone knows me?"

"Then Chico it is. I'll alert the world to drop the word 'Boy.' I think it's very appropriate as you seem to be growing up lately, what with your good grades and expanded vocabulary."

"Yeah, I'm definitely starting to get a lot better at English and math, thanks to Miss Lancer's help. If things keep going like they are, I may be a math whiz one day."

Gathering her things, she motioned for him to follow her toward the front door.

At just the moment she was preparing to exit, Chico's big sister, Debra, came in the door. With big, soft brown eyes like a doe and long, shiny, wheat-colored hair, Talula thought she was so cool looking. With a sense of awe, she watched as the older girl swept past them, hardly acknowledging their presence as she went to the kitchen.

Talula heard his sister rattling around in the background getting out a bag of chips from the pantry while she and Chico stood awkwardly at the door saying goodbye. If only she had half the sophistication of Debra, then her love life would be wonderful. But she didn't, so she squeaked out in a shy voice the only thing her tomboy-self could think of to say, which was "Call me when you finish checking out the trailer no matter how late." She had her own phone in her room. If she caught it on the first ring, her parent's wouldn't hear.

Chico heard them behind him as he entered the church parking lot. They must have followed him at a distance then moved forward quickly when they finally had him isolated. He heard their heavy panting as they half-ran up on his back. There was no need to turn around. He knew who they were.

"Hey, doofus." Chico always thought Randall's voice was high for a bully.

He mentally prepared to fight all three of them.

The one who had called him "doofus" was Randall and he was the largest. He outweighed Chico by thirty pounds and was a few inches taller. In his head, he liked to refer to Randall as Fat Boy. The other two were brothers that looked a lot alike, so much so it was difficult to tell them apart. The only distinguishing difference between them was one had a heavy mop of long dark hair and the other had a mop of short dark hair. Other than that they looked a lot like each other and a lot like many other fourteen year olds—skinny, tall, with the start of a bad acne problem. Chico referred to the brothers in his head as Ignoramus One and Ignoramus Two.

Fat Boy pulled the pink notebook out of Chico's bag. He started turning the pages looking at the math problems and creative writing samples. Chico reached out for the pink notebook and, as expected, Fat Boy punched him. Only this time it wasn't just one punch—it was a flurry of fists. Hatred boiled over out of every one of Fat Boy's pores. And the other two jumped in and held Chico's arms so he couldn't defend himself.

Then Fat Boy began to throw in all kinds of verbal slings, too, mostly about Chico's lack of intelligence. And the part that hurt the most is a lot of it was just plain true. Chico definitely lagged behind the rest of the kids his age. You can't hide stuff like this in a small town. And when you tried to change it—well, most people didn't want to let you, except for people like Miss Lancer, who actually tutored him for free here at the church.

Chico looked up in time to see Fat Boy pick up a big chunk of concrete in his right hand. As he drew back to throw it, a female hand appeared from behind his big body and stopped him. Next thing you know Fat Boy was rolling in the air before coming back down flat on his back. The two brothers shot a quick look up at Miss Lancer before they released Chico's arms and ran. She gave chase to them for a short distance yelling for them to stop.

Fat Boy took her distraction as an opportunity to escape as he ran off in the opposite direction of the twins. Chico could hardly stand. He watched as Miss Jillian Lancer, the only teacher he'd ever had a crush on, picked up his pink notebook and book bag. Only a few stray hairs had escaped her tidy ponytail. Her neon lime green polyester pantsuit remained wrinkle-free and her makeup looked fresh. The only sign that she'd just driven away Randall and the Ignoramus twins was a slight line of perspiration on her upper lip.

Be still my beating heart, Chico thought as she walked beside him toward the church's youth center. After they had entered the gymnasium, she turned and said, "Are you okay?"

"Yeah," he hesitated before adding, "Miss Lancer, can I ask you something?"

"What is it?" She looked at him with concern.

"I was wondering," he stopped and started again as he put his pink notebook down on one of the tables set-up for tutoring. "I was wondering if one day you might show me a few of those karate moves you did today?" Chico managed a smile at her. "You looked just like one of those female fighters on that new secret agent TV show. Didn't even mess your hair up."

"It's not Karate. It's Aiki, although I know Karate, too," she said as she retied and tightened the belt on her pantsuit. "Maybe I can get you into some martial arts classes at the Y."

"Does it cost money?"

"Or we can work on some moves at the end of each of our tutoring sessions."

` For one split second, his dream of riding the motorcycle up the meat mountain came back to him, and he remembered he was actually negotiating the squishy, bloody beef pretty well just before he woke up. The thought gave him hope for the future.

CHAPTER 2

The night was filled with crickets singing and other nocturnal wildlife running about. It didn't really bother Chico as he walked along the deserted country road toward the trailer. But he wished Big Mike could have come along.

He didn't dare wait another day as whoever got shot might still be alive. Lying there, writhing in pain while he and Talula tried to pretend it was firecrackers.

The weather-beaten trailer stood outlined against the bright silvery moon. Good. It looked as if no one was inside. Chico contemplated for a moment the best point of entry. Slowly, he made his way around from the front to the back. At the far back corner was a small plywood garden shed, positioned almost underneath what appeared to be a bedroom window.

Chico climbed up beside the window and listened. He considered breaking and opening it, but decided prying it would create less noise. Taking out his Swiss Army knife he began to work at the window until it popped up easily. Chico remembered seeing some of the windows open earlier that day, but now they were all closed. Whoever had shut them had done it in a hurry, not even bothering to lock up. Maybe they intended to come back and cleanup.

He stuck his head in first. Ouch. He hit his forehead in the same place he'd wounded it earlier. A small fairyland nightlight cast its glow in the corner of the room. That was the only thing childlike. The rest of the stuff looked to be hunting and fishing gear.

Wriggling his skinny behind through the window was easy, but one of Chico's large tennis shoes got stuck. He had to take the shoe off to get through. He smelled how stinky it was as he held it in his hand. They would just have to remain smelly until he got a new pair at the start of school. Another month and a half of "stink foot," as Talula would say.

He wished Talula were with him now.

Chico reached down and retrieved a flashlight that was left near the head of the bed. It was hard to maneuver in the faint glow of the nightlight. More than once he stubbed his toe in the unfamiliar surroundings.

When he got to the area in the den near the TV set, he stopped and waited before turning on the flashlight. Then, with a deep breath, he flipped the silver button under his thumb and illuminated the room in a ghostly haze. It was a good flashlight, a hunter's flashlight, stocked with fresh batteries.

Getting down on his knees, he discovered a dark stain on the green shag carpet.

Oil?

Maybe blood, but he didn't think so. It was very black.

Sitting back on his heels, he studied the fake paneling on the wall. There was a splintered bullet hole. He stared at it, willing it to be something else. But no, it was most probably a bullet hole.

Turning off the flashlight, he made his way to the back room by moonlight through the windows. It too was a bedroom. Or maybe more properly called a junk room. There were all sorts of gadgets in various stages of being worked on at a big desk. Some were kind of interesting, but Chico wanted to get out. As he turned to go back to the room he'd climbed through, he had a stellar thought. Why not use the front door?

And so he did.

Just as he thought he was home free, he looked up to see a pickup truck turning into the trailer's gravel drive. It had its lights off. If he had been listening, he would have heard it. But listening wasn't one of Chico's strong points.

All at once the driver flipped on their headlights, catching him by complete surprise. Leaping up like a deer, he bounded for the nearby woods.

Zigzagging across the narrow field, he ran for the cover of the looming tree line.

Pop. Pop. Two shots rang out.

He heard the sound of the first bullet as it narrowly missed him. And the second bullet whizzed in right behind it, a little more to the left. He pushed right and jumped into a small clump of bushes. On this hands and knees, he made fast time deep into the woods until he got to a small creek.

His heart thumped so hard and hurt so bad, he thought for a second one of the bullets had hit their mark. Holding his hand to his chest, he searched for the sticky feel of blood, but didn't find it. Then he rolled over on his back. His breath came in wheezes.

He needed to get his breathing under control so they wouldn't hear if they had followed him. Moving back to a sitting position, he concentrated on his breath. And he listened. He heard them talking at a distance. Then he heard the trailer door slam. Moving back toward the field but keeping down low, he saw they had turned the lights on in the trailer. The door was ajar and he could see two figures moving about. Turning, he headed deeper into the woods hoping to find his way out on the other side near a new subdivision of houses.

After a few moments, he stopped and listened again. He couldn't hear anything but the hum of small night creatures. A slight breeze washed over him, sending a little chill up his spine. He felt the cold steel of the mag flashlight from the trailer in his hand. Unbelievably, he had the presence of mind to keep holding on to it. Talula would've been impressed. Now he turned it on and the ominous shadows around him turned into saplings and tree trunks.

"Boy, don't turn that light on yet," a deep voice whispered from somewhere to his right.

Chico returned to panic mode, frantically searching the direction the voice had come from with his bright beam of light.

Pushed up against a tree trunk was a wounded man. His thick hair matted down with sweat, his skin too pale to be okay. Through bluish lips, he whispered something that sounded like, "I'm not the bad guy."

Chico saw blood on the man's upper left shirtsleeve. It looked like he had wrapped some sort of dishtowel around it, but the blood had seeped through that as well. Shielding his eyes from the bright flashlight beam, the man began struggling to get to his feet.

"Help me." He lumbered toward Chico.

Fear seized Chico's heart and he moved away from the man's outstretched arm. Turning, he ran across the small creek and headed toward home. Tears formed in his eyes and snot ran from his nose. The moon lit his way. He couldn't get involved. He wanted to turn his life around. Being in situations where you get shot at twice was not turning things around.

For a moment, Chico contemplated why this man had a bullet wound. Obviously, he was the victim of this afternoon's events. Did he owe a gambling debt? Had he made them mad cheating? Was it a bad drug deal? All the reasons someone might shoot you for were not good.

Stopping to catch his breath, he gazed upward. A bright three-quarter moon slipped out from behind clouds and lit the sky as guilt overcame him. Turning, he ran back to help the man.

He didn't have to go to far. The stranger had managed to stumble forward through the woods on his own. Chico walked toward him and looped the man's good arm over his shoulder. The relief in the man's eyes let Chico know he had made the right decision. But the look of relief was only there momentarily before pain clouded it again.

Chico held the flashlight in his free hand. The man made no mention of the light being on this time. Together they made their way toward town, neither saying a word.

Whether the wounded man wanted to go or not, Chico had already decided he was going to take him to the pastor's house. Brother Lowe would take him to the hospital without questions. Chico had gotten to know the pastor pretty well since he was taking after-school tutoring sessions with Miss Lancer at the church. Much to his surprise, Brother Lowe often stopped by the sessions to see how things were progressing and more than a few times he had helped him solve a difficult math problem.

Suffice it to say, Chico wasn't used to having people interested in him. Most adults barely gave him a second glance. But Brother Lowe was a really nice person and that's why he felt like he could take the wounded man to him.

He was certain he could find the pastor's house in the subdivision because his tutor, Miss Lancer, actually lived across the street from the church and so did Brother Lowe. One day after lessons, she had pointed out both of their houses. Of course, she had said she rented hers because she would be getting married soon. Miss Lancer liked to talk about getting married a lot. At the time, he couldn't imagine how she afforded the new home on a substitute teacher's salary. He had always wanted to live in a house like hers, but for now he was happy his family had their trailer.

As he walked through the night with the stranger leaning heavily on him, he tried to remember the quickest shortcut to their houses. Probably the alley would be best. He cut off the flashlight as they came out of the woods. The glow of streetlights beckoned up ahead.

"What's your name?" The stranger struggled to talk.

"Allen," Chico said.

Intuitively, he knew he didn't want to know too much about the man and he didn't want the man to know too much about him. All he wanted was to get him help and get away from the situation. His mother didn't need any more problems in her life. His dad had caused her enough. And Chico intended to make it up to her. To make her proud he was her son.

"I'm going to take you to Brother Lowe's house," Chico said. "He's the pastor of the church. He'll know how to help you." The man said nothing. So Chico continued, "I'm a kid. I can't take you to the hospital."

21

"I can't go to the hospital." The man's voice was low and grim. Not angry, but laced with pain. "We can part ways here."

Chico had already steered him up the alley toward Brother Lowe's house.

"I can't leave you here. It's only a little ways more."

The man pulled back. "I've got a friend I can call."

"Call him from Brother Lowe's."

Just then the two of them heard the sound of someone running. Both immediately stopped talking and retreated to the shadows.

A lone form jogged down the alley toward them. As the runner got closer Chico could make out the person's face in the pale moonlight.

"Miss Lancer?"

He could tell by the way she jumped and let out a small scream that he had scared her.

She slowed, but didn't stop. "Chico? What are you doing in my alley?"

Chico didn't know how to respond without frightening her further. The man with the gunshot wound hid himself behind some trashcans.

"Chico? Are you doing something with the trashcans?" Her voice was tense.

"No, I'm over here."

"Is someone with you?"

"Yes, it's a man. He's hurt. I was bringing him to Brother Lowe's."

Miss Lancer had stopped. He saw she had her hands on her knees as she caught her breath. It occurred to him she must have been in a hurry to get somewhere or away from someone.

"Miss Lancer, do you mind me asking why you're running in the alley?"

"For exercise."

Chico had heard it all now. She was out running in the dark for exercise? He'd heard of people running for exercise, but mostly high school athletes, not substitute teachers.

The man came out of the shadows, and Miss Lancer gasped again.

"I don't think you have to be afraid of him." Chico tried to calm her. "He's lost a lot of blood from his gunshot wound. He's too weak to hurt you."

"I'm not afraid Chico," she said, her voice level. "I know this person."

Chico's heart lurched. He was shocked to his core that she knew the wounded man, a guy who had done something so bad people had felt the need to shoot him for it.

"He's my brother, Ben." Miss Lancer said without emotion.

Chico was so surprised by this last comment that he almost fell over his own two feet as he backed away from the two of them.

Stammering, he forgot his grammar. "He don't look like you."

It was true. She was slender with straight dark hair and brown eyes, while the man she called Ben was large and burly with wavy reddish-brown hair and green eyes. They even had different accents: his Texan, hers Midwest.

"Ben is my brother," Miss Lancer announced again as if she said it out loud enough times everyone would believe it to be the truth.

Chico didn't want to call anyone a liar, but…

"Help me get him inside my house." Miss Lancer put Ben's arm around her neck to help him walk. "Then go get Brother Lowe—he was an army medic at one time.

He'll know what to do about Ben's injury."

"Shouldn't we take him to the hospital?" Chico asked in amazement as he watched the petite woman hoist the large man up off the ground.

"Not unless we have to." Miss Lancer guided the man who was supposed to be her brother up the alley toward her house. "Now go get Brother Lowe and tell him we need his help A.S.A.P. I'm counting on you, Chico. Don't let me down."

Looking at his watch, Chico saw it was almost ten-thirty. "Brother Lowe might be asleep," he thought as he rang the doorbell.

But, no, the light over the front porch turned on a few seconds later. Then someone started unlocking the front door. And it opened a crack.

Chico saw Brother Lowe's kindly face peep out. The chain came off its hook and the door opened fully, revealing the pastor's tall, muscular frame.

Unlike Miss Lancer, Brother Lowe seemed accustomed to people showing up unannounced, out-of-nowhere, late at night, and with a problem.

"Do you need to talk with me?" Brother Lowe said in a gentle tone.

"Miss Lancer needs you . . . at her house."

"What's wrong?" The preacher asked, his voice slightly panicked.

Chico said, "I don't even know how to start to tell the story. But a man's been shot."

Soon enough they were on Miss Lancer's porch and she was leading them both inside. Cautiously, she took

Brother Lowe by the arm and whispered something to him. Chico couldn't hear even though he strained his ears hard.

Ben was stretched out on some clean blankets on the kitchen floor. Brother Lowe kneeled beside him and started an examination. Miss Lancer threw a worried glance at the clock.

"Shouldn't you be home by now, Chico? Your mother will be worried." Miss Lancer picked up her purse. "Let me drive you home. You shouldn't be involved in this. Did anyone see you helping my brother?"

"No . . . maybe." He thought about telling her they shot at him twice. "I don't think they could tell you what I looked like."

"Good. Let's get you home."

"No, I'll walk. I like to walk." Really, he was going to run. His mom would be home from the late shift soon and would start to call around looking for him. Hopefully, Big Mike or Talula wouldn't tell her. He didn't want her driving out to the trailer this time of night.

With a glance over at Ben's outstretched form, he watched the pastor, who had just washed his hands, begin to tenderly inspect the wound. As he opened the door and stepped out, he overheard Brother Lowe say, "It's superficial. Jillian. Is the water you have boiling ready?"

"Yes," he heard Miss Lancer reply. "And I have plenty of clean bandages and alcohol." Then much to his surprise, he heard her add, "Did either of you get a chance to look at the wedding veil pictures?" And even more surprising, Ben answered, "I think I like the one with the tiara," just before he let out a groan and a shriek.

"Sorry," Brother Lowe said softly before continuing, "Jillian, I think you should wear the wildflower wreath you showed us last week instead of a veil. Hand me more bandages, please."

For someone who knew Aiki and Karate and was a bit of a tomboy, Miss Lancer sure was into planning her wedding. *Her wedding.* Chico sighed as he closed the door behind him and hurried down the porch steps looking both ways to make certain no one saw or followed him.

It was an easy run home.

His mom had just gotten home and was waiting up for him, reading a magazine in the den. Relief flooded her face. She didn't say anything negative, only hugged him goodnight and told him how much she loved him.

He watched her walk down the hall toward her room. She knocked on his sister's door as she passed and told her to get off the phone. He heard Debra saying good-bye to her latest boyfriend.

Good. He would be able to call Talula.

Moving into the kitchen, he carefully picked up the phone's receiver and listened for a dial tone. Dragging the rotary dial, he called Talula. She answered on half a ring.

"Yes?" her anxious voice whispered.

"It was fireworks. I found boxes and boxes of fireworks."

She started to giggle. "I can't believe your overactive imagination."

"Yeah, crazy thinking someone got shot."

"You know what?" Talula said. "I got out that little dream interpretation book I bought at the grocery store and it says raw meat is symbolic of obstacles to be overcome."

Chico held his breath. "Yeah, and that's probably talking about like one steak or something. I was riding on a mountain of raw meat."

Talula snorted a laugh. "So you got a few problems in your life, do you?"

"Not problems. Obstacles." Chico was smiling now, but he kept his voice low. "I have to go. See you tomorrow."

"Bye."

"Bye," he whispered as he heard his mom come back down the hallway.

"Who are you on the phone with this late?" His mother said.

"Big Mike." Chico didn't want her asking questions about why he would call Talula so late. In his most chipper voice, he continued his fib. "Seems Miss Lancer wants us to go to church camp next week."

His mother's face lit up. "Church camp . . . maybe I can afford . . ."

"Miss Lancer said the church would cover the fee for me. She's already looked into it since she is officially in charge of chaperoning us kids."

"Well, I'll call and thank her. Still, we'll have to buy you a few things."

"I don't need anything." He knew how tight money was, and it was really tight this summer because she wasn't getting as many hours at her waitressing job.

"You need underwear, Chico. You can't go to church camp without underwear."

The thought of new underwear was a good one. He'd like that. But he wasn't so sure about going to church camp. Why had he used that as an excuse for being on the phone? Now his mom was going to call Miss Lancer and he couldn't get out of it. Miss Lancer would be pleased he'd decided to go. Every female in his life was going to be pleased, including Talula because her mother was making her go. Sitting on the side of his bed, he contemplated taking a second shower before going to sleep when his mother came to his door.

"So what did Big Mike say?"

"About what?"

"Church camp. Is he going?

"Yeah, yeah he's going."

His mother reached up and turned off the light. "You two are going to have so much fun. I don't think you've had a vacation since before your dad left."

Dark thoughts crowded his mind as he thought of his dad's sudden departure. It was a shock as his parents hardly ever fought. In fact, he felt like they had a very loving relationship. The few memories he had of his father were those of a good guy. He would never believe his father didn't love his mother or him and his sister. But his mom kept telling him to tell anyone who asked that their dad left them. But to him, his dad abandoning them did not make sense. All he had to go on was one conversation he had overheard of his father telling his mother that his job was just too dangerous right now to stay. What kind of job did his dad have? Whenever he asked his mother, she just said she didn't want to talk about it. Maybe when he was older she'd open up.

Soon, Chico's thoughts returned to the ordeal he'd just been through. He couldn't believe the men at the trailer had shot at him. Maybe getting out of town for a week wouldn't be so bad; no one was going to kill a kid at church camp. Or at least he hoped not.

CHAPTER 3

Talula could hardly sleep. She reviewed her list of things needed for church camp. She had looked at it so much, she almost had it memorized. It was exciting enough to be going away from home for a week, but the fact that Chico was going with her—a minor miracle. They were going to have a great time.

Since she couldn't sleep, she got up to check her suitcase one more time.

Then, to her surprise, her phone rang. She reached out and grabbed it on one ring.

"Hello," she whispered, glancing at the clock.

It was Chico. "I can't sleep."

"I can't sleep either. I'm so excited."

"You're excited? Excuse my language, but church camp is going to be boring as heck."

"It is?"

"Yeah, just a bunch of preaching."

Talula contemplated this for a moment. All she had thought of was swimming and horseback riding and being away from home for a week. She hadn't thought of nonstop preaching.

"I guess we can act sick in the morning and stay home."

"No, we'll go. We can think of fun stuff to do while the preaching's going on."

"Besides, Big Mike says church girls are hot."

Talula's heart sank.

Chico didn't wait for her response; he continued right on, not even noticing the hurt he was causing. "But I told Big Mike what's the use if they're good-looking, if they're church girls? They won't want to do anything."

"You mean like make-out? At church camp?"

Then he shocked her again by saying, "My mom bought me new underwear."

"That was nice of her."

"Yeah, she couldn't really afford it. But she said I needed to wear it because it was church camp."

"She's kind of right." Talula was thinking about him segueing from making out with girls to new underwear. Good thing his mom did buy it or those church girls would be shocked. But she really thought he and Big Mike would be lucky if they got a girl to kiss them. They were all talk.

Looking at her reflection in the mirror, Talula reached up and swept her long brown hair out of her eyes. Sometimes she thought Chico talked about other girls to make her jealous. Or maybe he still hadn't figured out she liked him. She hadn't told anyone. Maybe he was trying to get a reaction out of her. Well, she would show him. He hadn't hurt her.

"I hope there are a lot of cute guys there. This girl in my Sunday School class says the guys from the Midlothian area are the cutest guys in the world." Talula waited to see what he would say.

"Hey, are you going to bring an autograph book?" Chico seemed to be ignoring her last comment on purpose. At first she thought about calling him on it, then she decided to let it slide.

"Yeah. Maybe. I need to get one."

"Big Mike and I couldn't figure out why it was on the list of things to bring. I mean. whose autograph are we going to get at church camp? Jesus'?" Talula laughed at his joke and it just egged him on. "Maybe Moses'? Or Judas'?" Talula giggled again a little too loud.

Her mother's voice called out from her parent's bedroom, "Talula, are you on the phone?"

Chico said a quick goodbye and hung up just as she answered her mother. "No, I had a funny dream and I guess I laughed out loud in my sleep."

"What was your dream about, honey?" Her mom's voice sounded only half awake.

"Jesus signing autograph books at church camp."

It was really hard to get up. Chico had put the alarm clock far away from the bed so he would actually have to get out of bed and walk across the room to turn it off. But now it was morning, and he didn't want to wake up this early. He hid his head underneath his pillow as the alarm kept up its obnoxiously loud beeping sound. Finally, his mother came in and turned it off.

"Come on. Get up." She gently pulled on his arm.

He sat up in bed.

She gestured to his clothes hanging on a chair near his desk. "Just slip them on. I'll make your breakfast."

Chico looked up at her. For the first time it hit him that she was worried about him being away from home. Her face was strained and there was worry in her eyes. He thought back to the two bullets that whizzed by him the other night. He had been thinking of his mother as he zigzagged across the field into the woods, how she wouldn't be able to live without him and Debra.

Now that their father was gone, she lived her life for them. After his dad left, she never accepted any dates. And she was a nice-looking woman. She got offers, but she always said her dating days were behind her. It made him sad to think of her giving up on love at her young age.

He stood up and went into the bathroom. First he peed and then washed his hands, splashing cold water over his face. Now he was wide awake and ready to begin the trip to church camp.

His mom was in the kitchen making French toast. She must really be worried about his leaving. Usually she was wasted flat out from waitressing so many hours and all she could manage was cereal. He hadn't had French toast since the first day of first grade.

Chico put on his new underwear. "You can't help but feel good when you put on new underwear," he thought. "Especially when you haven't had any in two years." Next came his jeans. The good ones with only a tiny hole in them. And then his t-shirt and tennis shoes. He realized his mom had washed the stinky sneakers in spite of his protests and they'd held up, but just barely.

Big Mike's mom had mentioned Big Mike was outgrowing his new tennis shoes already. So she'd asked Chico if he wanted them when she got Mike some new ones. Maybe she'd gotten him new ones for church camp. Chico could only hope.

"Do you want some milk?" Chico's mom asked as she handed him the French toast.

He noticed she'd sprinkled powdered sugar on top

just like they did down at the restaurant.

"Sure."

"And I packed you a sack lunch for the bus ride." She put the sack near the door with his suitcase. Then she went over to her purse on the couch. She pulled out twenty dollars. "Here's some spending money."

Chico stared at the wrinkled twenty in her hand.

"I don't need money."

"Yes, you do, for snacks. And souvenirs."

"No, I won't be buying souvenirs. Put it back in your purse."

She walked over to his suitcase and zipped it into the outside pocket. "Just in case," she said. "Just in case you have an emergency."

Chico watched as his sister, Debra, came into the kitchen. Yawning, she took out a cereal bowl, but when she saw the French toast, her sleepy eyes lit up. "Wow, French toast. Things are going to be nice around here with you gone, little brother."

He knew his sister loved him even though she put him down constantly.

Looking up at the clock above the stove, he realized he needed to move it. Big Mike's mom would be coming by to pick him up soon. Finishing the last bite of toast, he went into the bathroom and brushed his teeth again. He liked the feeling of clean teeth.

Outside, a car horn honked.

He hugged and kissed his mom good-bye. Then he went over to Debra. Reluctantly, she offered him the side of her face to kiss. He licked it like a dog instead and she kicked him. She was still kicking him when he was going down the metal front steps of their trailer.

Big Mike and his mom, who was also big, were waving at him with happy smiles on their faces. They already had the trunk popped to put his suitcase inside. As he went around to the back, Big Mike's mom called out to him. "I put those shoes I told you about in the trunk in case you wanted to wear them." Chico looked down and saw them. They were hardly worn. And they were the good kind of tennis shoes. The kind he would never be able to afford.

Putting his suitcase inside, he hoped against hope the tennis shoes weren't way too big. Size 8 the interior toe tag read. He held them in his right hand and shut the trunk with his left. He hardly had the back car door closed before he ripped off his old shoes and put the new ones on. They were only a little too large. If he laced them really tight they would work.

"A perfect fit." He announced to Big Mike's mom. "Thank you."

"Good. Now I know my money didn't go to waste. His foot outgrew those shoes after only a month." Big Mike's mom talked up to the rearview mirror instead of turning around.

Hot dog! He smiled to himself at this latest turn of good fortune. *New underwear and new tennis shoes. Life's looking up.*

Moving his old shoes to the other side of the floorboard, he noticed he could smell their stink even though his mom had just washed them. And he saw the rubber sole was parting from the upper canvas. Grass stains and tiny holes graced the rotting material even though he'd tried to keep them in good condition. He wanted to ask Big Mike's mom to throw them away, but he was afraid to get rid of them yet. They'd make a good backup pair when he was doing yard work and stuff. He wondered if he put them in his suitcase if his clothes would stink. Probably. He would just leave them in the back. And if they were still there when she took him home next week, he would get them then.

"Did you bring an autograph book?" Big Mike's Mom asked Chico. She was looking at him in the rearview mirror again. And this time she was also applying lipstick.

"No, ma'am."

"See, Mom? I told you I didn't need one," Big Mike scolded her.

"Well, I bought two—one for each of you." She paused before continuing, "It was on the list of things to bring, so it must be important."

Chico couldn't see how it would be important, but he was touched she had bought him one, too. "Thank you," he said. "And thanks again for the tennis shoes. I really like them," he said as he looked down admiring the like-new leather.

Big Mike turned around in the front seat and said, "I'm starting to get excited about going somewhere." And Chico realized he was, too.

Talula's mind was going a mile a minute as her mother pulled the car into the church parking lot. A big yellow bus idled in the middle of the crowd of excited campers as their hurried parents gave last minute hugs. Suitcases were scattered everywhere as their owners dropped them to the ground before going off to talk to their friends. The colorful chaos looked like a school carnival more than an organized church outing. Sensing her anxiety, her mother leaned over and patted her hand. Then she parked the car, and they got out.

Talula's stomach did a somersault. The melee left her breathless as she searched frantically for Chico. And when she couldn't find him, she panicked. What if he had chickened out?

Then she spotted Big Mike. His mom was hugging him. Then Big Mike stepped back and Talula saw Chico getting his suitcase out of the car. Talula's heart jumped the way it always did when she saw Chico.

"Lord, that boy is handsome," Talula's mother said, glancing over in Chico's direction.

"You're embarrassing me. Stop talking." Talula gave her mother a mean glare. "Now."

Chico saw them looking his way and his face lit up, Talula thought not unlike her dog Cassie, a German shepherd mix. Every time Cassie saw Talula, her eyes took on a sparkling glow as she charged over for a good pet on the head while she walked around Talula's legs, almost tripping her. Even as she thought the thought Chico charged towards them. Big Mike was following close behind. Talula braced herself for their arrival.

"See, I told you he liked you," Talula's mom held her hand over her mouth and said it low enough only Talula could hear.

"Mother, people might hear you."

Before Chico and Big Mike reached them, someone blew a whistle. It was Miss Lancer. She had two purple flowered suitcases beside her and a pile of bridal magazines on top. Stepping to the side of her suitcases, she blew the whistle again. Only this time harder and everyone stopped and paid attention.

"Listen up!" she yelled to the crowd of excited kids. "It's time to start boarding the bus. When I call your name, say, 'Here,' and get on the bus. Leave your suitcases in this pile," she pointed to her purple cases, "to be loaded on the bus."

No one said a word as it was clear Miss Lancer was in charge. She called name after name and the kids loaded in an orderly manner onto the bus. Chico and Big Mike were some of the first ones called, right along with Randall. "Oh, no," Talula said to her mother. "That's the kid that bullies Chico. What's he doing here?"

"Camp will probably do him good," her mother replied as she brushed Talula's hair out of her face.

Talula stood nervously and waited.

Finally, Miss Lancer called her name. "Talula Moonstone," she yelled over the pinging sounds of the bus's engine.

A few giggles were heard. It was always the same.

Even though everyone knew she had the weirdest name in the world, they always laughed when it was called out loud. But, as her father had pointed out, no matter what name they put with Moonstone, it was going to sound weird.

If only she could marry Chico, then her last name would be Campbell. Mrs. Richard Campbell. Talula Clarice Campbell. She'd written it secretly over and over again.

Her mother gave her a kiss on the cheek and a little push toward the idling bus. Its noxious fumes, along with the anxiety of being away from home, made her stomach a little nauseous.

As she climbed aboard the first steel step, she found herself at eye level with the bus driver's boots, snakeskin boots. Her heart gave a jump. A roar came to her ears. She swallowed hard. Even though she had only opened her eyes for a moment in the horse shed, she'd never forget those snakeskin boots or the deep gruff voice that went with them.

Quickly, she averted her eyes and continued down the bus aisle. Chico had saved her a seat. Big Mike was sitting in a seat by himself.

Sitting down by Chico, she willed her heart to beat normally. Why was she so upset? Chico had said he found fireworks. Lots and lots of fireworks. But she knew deep in her heart that if it had only been fireworks, the two men wouldn't have come over to the shed trying to make sure no one heard. What were two kids going to do? Turn them in? They'd be more likely to steal the rest of the fireworks and keep them for themselves. But the men hadn't found them in the shed that day, and no one had seen Chico when he went back. So they were probably okay.

Suddenly, Big Mike's mom appeared at the front of the bus, holding up Chico's old sneakers. She waved them around in the air, and Chico immediately jumped up and ran to her.

Smiling, she said, "They haven't put your suitcase on the bus. If you hurry you can put them in it."

Chico thanked her and grabbed his shoes as he scooted past her going out the bus door. Once outside, he made record time getting the shoes to his suitcase. Unzipping the front pocket, he saw the twenty his mom had put in earlier that morning. Taking it out, he pressed the two old canvas track shoes as flat as he could get them inside before zipping it back up. Big Mike's mom stood and waited. As he got up, she smiled at him and held out her arms for one more good-bye hug.

"Now, you two boys be good, you hear?" She squished him in a bear hug and her sweet flowery perfume wafted over him, killing the still lingering scent of his old sneakers.

"Oh, I'm sure they will." It was the bus driver. He was standing just outside the bus door watching them. "You can trust me to keep an eye on old Chico Boy here."

The bus driver had his handkerchief out now and was polishing a little red dust off his boot tip. He looked up and caught Chico's eye before giving him an insincere smile.

Chico tried not to stare at the man's snakeskin boots as he pocketed the wrinkled twenty-dollar bill he was still holding in his hand. For emergencies. Isn't that what his mother had said?

CHAPTER 4

Talula watched Chico coming down the aisle toward her on the bus. He had the strangest look on his face. Immediately, she knew he knew about the driver wearing the snakeskin boots. But she also knew Chico thought she had her eyes clamped shut through the whole ordeal in the shed. So should she tell him she saw the snakeskin boots? He would only tell her it was firecrackers again. But then again, she didn't like the startled look on his face. She should let him know so he wouldn't feel so alone. Like he had to carry this thing by himself.

She decided not to say anything about it though, and she rode without speaking as Chico and Big Mike joked with each other. For some time they talked about motorcycles and cars and lots of other guy stuff, not seeming to give her another thought. Then Chico interrupted her rambling mind as he turned his attention to her.

"What are you so preoccupied with?" he said, reaching out to touch her arm.

Thinking fast, she said, "Another animal story."

Big Mike leaned over from the seat behind them and said, "What's this one about?"

"A little dog." She was grasping for something to answer. She had forgotten Big Mike liked her animal stories.

Chico made himself comfortable in the seat and said, "So, shoot."

"What do you mean 'shoot'?" Talula stammered.

"Shoot. Start. Tell the animal story."

Talula didn't have a new animal story, and she couldn't revise one she'd previously told because Big Mike never forgot anything. He'd call her on it for sure. She would have to improvise and make up something new. Stalling for time, she turned her back to the window and tucked her legs up on the seat. This way she could easily talk to Big Mike and Chico at the same time. She watched as Big Mike leaned forward in anticipation.

Then, in her best storyteller voice, she began, loud enough so those near her could hear, but not so loud that everyone else on the bus would. Chico turned sideways in his seat to listen. Her heart leapt when he let his hand fall nonchalantly on the back of the bus seat near her. Even though her heart was doing a little fluttery thing, she started telling the story.

"Blue was a part-time dog . . . and a part-time angel." She paused to let this sink in to their collective minds before continuing. "Most of the time Blue was your regular friendly dog that liked to do doglike activities such as eating milk bones, digging holes and chewing on stuff. But sometimes when his owner, Henry, needed extra help. He was an angel, a real guardian angel sent down from heaven. In fact, there was a special window in the sky the guardian angel slipped in and out of. Once on earth, he would jump into Blue's body and they'd share it

41

for a while."

"Wait, I have to ask a question." Big Mike's forehead was scrunched up as he looked very seriously at Talula. "Is this a true story?"

Swatting at Big Mike, Chico laughed and said, "Of course not."

"Well, it's sort of true in here's-another-fact-I-just-made-up way."

"It's all in her imaginary world, Big Mike," Chico said as he gave Talula a slight thump on the head. "Just because she lives there doesn't mean the rest of us do."

Big Mike shifted in his seat and leaned forward so he was hanging over the back of their seat. "Well, before we were even in kindergarten, Talula used to have a dog named Blue so I thought I needed to ask."

"Before kindergarten you had a dog named Blue that was part German Shepherd and part guardian angel and you never told me?" Chico sounded incredulous.

"I must have told you at some time because I never said in my story he was part German Shepherd." Talula looked funny. "I think you're psychic, Chico."

"No, if I were psychic, I would have said what other breed of dog Blue was, such as Border Collie or Golden Retriever . . ."

Big Mike and Talula gasped in horror, stopping Chico's little tirade short.

"Blue was part Border Collie and part Golden Retriever," Big Mike looked truly shaken.

Talula couldn't help but add, "And, of course, part guardian angel."

"I wonder what else Chico knows that he's holding out on us." Big Mike said these last words a little too loud. Talula looked up just in time to see Chico meet the bus driver's eyes in the rearview mirror. From her vantage point, neither one looked too happy.

Suddenly, the bus took a sharp right. The bus driver didn't slow down enough and the bus seemed to be on two wheels for a few seconds. All the kids grabbed the seats and hung on for dear life. Talula found herself in Chico's lap. He held on to her with one hand and the railing on the seat in front of them with the other. Pandemonium and screaming followed as the bus righted itself and screeched to a halt.

Talula turned beet red as Chico jokingly said to her, "Please, you don't have to fall all over me. If you wanted to make out, just ask." Climbing over him, she scrambled all the way to the other side of the bus to retrieve her purse from the floorboard.

As the kids tried to gather their wits, the bus driver stood up in the aisle and turned around to face them. In a very calm voice he announced the bus was stopping for lunch at the Dairy Royal for thirty minutes. He then walked down the steps of the bus and toward the restaurant. Talula couldn't help but notice he stopped to polish the toe of his snakeskin boots before going in the front door.

When Chico turned back to look at Talula, he saw her watching Mr. Snakeskin Boots, too. By the look on her face, he was fairly certain she hadn't had her eyes clenched shut the whole time they were in the horse's shed. One side of him wished he had found out more about the wounded guy so he could discuss it with Talula, and the other side wanted to keep her totally out of it. Miss Lancer and Brother Lowe had been adamant about getting him off to church camp so he wouldn't be involved. If they were worried about him, they'd really be worried about Talula. He'd discuss the fact with Miss Lancer that he believed Snakeskin was her brother's shooter whenever he found the right time, and now was not the right time to tell anybody anything, including Talula.

Looking around for his sack lunch, he grabbed it and put it under his shirt so he could sneak it in the restaurant. Then he lined up with the others standing in the bus aisle waiting to get off and go inside the Dairy Royal.

Their church group hardly had time to get off the bus, get their food, and sit down when another busload of kids going to church camp stopped at the same place. The arriving bus was colorful with "Parkview Church" written in rainbow letters down the side of it. Underneath it were the words "Wolfe Town." Chico looked at his watch. They had fifteen minutes to eat. Stuffing his mouth as fast as he could with his mother's homemade sandwich, he noticed the Parkview Church bus had a lot of pretty girls. He tried not to gawk as he watched them get off the bus through the big plate glass window. And he tried to be cool when Talula said to him between bites of greasy hamburger, "You'd think coming from a place named Wolfe Town they'd be a lot uglier." But so much for being cool—he and Big Mike both turned to look back over their shoulders at the girls entering the door of the restaurant.

"I can't believe their church lets them wear shorts like that to church camp," Big Mike whispered to Chico. Chico smiled secretly back at Big Mike, and the two gave each other a discreet high five. Talula pretended not to notice.

Suddenly, one of the most un-wolf-like girls looked toward Chico and Big Mike. Recognition dawned in her face and her big cheerleader smile became even broader. Chico, Big Mike, and Talula watched as if in a dream as the girl grabbed the food she'd just paid for from the counter and ran in their direction. Sitting her tray at the occupied booth across from them, she reached out and hugged Chico to her ample bosom. "Oh, Chico Boy. How are you?"

Chico couldn't answer because she had his face squished into her chest.

"I don't think he can talk," Talula said to the girl, motioning toward Chico's captured head. "Maybe you should let him breathe."

Laughing, the girl released Chico and turned to sit down at the occupied booth by them. "Mind if I sit here?" There were only two boys sitting in the booth, and the one on her side moved down the bench-type chair to accommodate her. Both boys stared at her as she motioned three more cheerful girls with cute haircuts and perfect makeup to join her.

"Over here," she said. "I found us a place to sit." Turning to the two boys, she mouthed, "You don't mind, do you?" It was obvious they didn't by the way they made room for her and the other girls. In fact, one of the two guys gathered the girls' trays after they took their food off and the other one went for napkins and ketchup.

Chico looked confused as the girl hugged him up again. "You don't know who I am, do you?"

Everyone in the Dairy Royal waited for his reply. His mouth was full of Talula's leftover french fries. It was obvious he didn't know the girl by name from the embarrassed look on his face.

"I know who you are." Chico heard Big Mike sputter out the words. "You're Little Janie."

Relief flooded Chico's face.

The girl came over again and this time he stood up and hugged her. Chico looked down at his feet and said, "Sorry, didn't recognize you. You don't look like Little Janie anymore."

"But we still look alike, don't we?" The girl said as she pushed her face against Chico's. And he had to admit they did resemble. Only their hair color was very different.

"Everyone, this is my cousin Chico Boy that I haven't seen since I was about three years old. We used to do everything together, even bathe and take naps, and now he doesn't remember me." All the girls at the table started giggling as if the image of Chico and Janie bathing together were the funniest thing ever.

One more girl, the last to get her order, arrived and pushed into the booth beside Talula without asking. Chico watched from across the table as Talula scooted down to make room for her. Then, in a surprising move, the late arrival popped out of her seat and reached across to touch Chico on the head. "Dibs, this one is mine."

All the girls started giggling again. And all the guys stared as the recent arrival adjusted her too-short shorts before sitting back down near Talula.

Then one of the other girls jumped up and leaned over Chico to touch Big Mike on the head. Her mouth was full of food as she said, "Dibs on this one." And the other two girls turned and touched the heads of the two boys at their booth.

Chico tried to catch Talula's eye to see what she was thinking, but Talula was listening to not-so-little Janie whispering in her ear. He thought he heard her say, "We two are going to have to act fast if we don't want to end up alone." And his heart felt a little pang as Talula answered her, "I'm sure there'll be lots of better looking guys to choose from when we get there, Janie. By the way, we dropped 'Boy' off your cousin's name. Everyone just calls him Chico now."

Janie looked over and smiled at him. "Yes, he is growing up fast. Last time I saw him, I was taller than him. Now, he towers overs me. I think it's probably time to drop 'Boy' off."

Talula sat quietly and stared out the window as their bus rolled along. The passing countryside was pretty, at least. No one was talking to her. Well, that wasn't exactly true. Chico's cousin Janie was sitting beside her and she had tried to strike up a conversation twice, but it was just too much to respond back. Talula was madder than a wet hedgehog that the five Wolfe Town girls had asked to get on their bus. They had begged their chaperones to let them switch buses because theirs had been too crowded. "Too crowded my foot," she thought. Clearly these heathen girls felt the need to spread out and take over the Rivercrest Church bus and all the boys on it.

True, their bus had been only half full. Talula supposed this was because their small town wasn't as religious as the small town to their north. In her mind, Talula dubbed the Wolfe Town girls the "*Del Norte Women*"—translation: "Women of the North." She considered them the bane of her existence, although not-so-little Janie seemed to be trying to make friends. How could Talula be friends with her when every time she looked at her face she saw a glimmer of Chico?

Chico looked over at the seat his cousin Janie and Talula were sitting in. He was happy to see them getting along. If you could call Janie talking and Talula listening getting along, then they were going to be best friends. He missed sitting beside Talula. After all, technically she was his best friend. He had tried to make it more, but she had always been so shy when it came to boyfriend/girlfriend stuff. Maybe it was better to have a girlfriend like the one sitting next to him. She was the outgoing kind. But still, he missed his best friend.

Glancing back at Talula again, he saw she was trying to get his attention. She kept jerking her head as if to say, "Look toward the back of the bus." He did, but he couldn't see anything. In fact, the last seat looked completely empty. He lifted his hands as if to say, "What?"

Talula pointed to the back again.

"What's she saying?" The girl who had claimed him as hers at the Dairy Royal suddenly became possessive. Her name was Wanda Wright she had told him, ". . . as in the Wright woman for you." At least she had a sense of humor to go along with her incredible figure, and her face was more than decent.

Chico looked back over at Talula. She pointed at the back again.

"Look." Wanda pointed in the same direction as Talula.

This time Chico saw Big Mike's head pop up. "What's he doing?"

Wanda motioned for him to look down the aisle. Chico leaned over and looked. He saw Big Mike's legs and female legs hanging out of the aisle in the back seat of the bus. Wanda took his hand and whispered in his ear, "They're kissing. On the church bus."

Chico laughed.

Then she pulled him down in the seat, but he

popped right back up. She pulled him down again. "We can't kiss here," he said, unsure of himself as she pulled him close. Then their lips were touching and she was so soft. "Okay," he thought. "Just one kiss then I'll get back up." He didn't want Talula to see.

After cutting the kiss way too short, he sat back up. He looked over at Talula and saw her staring out the window. He felt pretty sure she didn't see, but that didn't make him feel better. He felt bad all the way down to the pit that was forming in his stomach.

Leaning forward, he got his cousin Janie's attention. "Let me sit by Talula for a minute."

"Okay," Janie got up and came back to switch seats.

Wanda held onto his arm, and Chico tried to be charming when he said, "I need to tell my friend Talula something."

Settling into the hard bus seat beside Talula, Chico felt his heart sinking. She didn't turn and say anything to him when he said, "Hey, Talula." She just stared out the window. So he hung his head down and sat beside her. Why did he feel guilty? She never acted like she wanted him to kiss her. His thoughts were of the troubled kind when suddenly Talula turned and whispered, "I don't think the guy with the snakeskin boots recognized us."

But in his heart, Chico knew he had. They'd been out in the bright sunlight feeding Silver for some time before they heard the gunshots in the trailer. Mr. Snakeskin had time to get a good look at them.

CHAPTER 5

Chico enjoyed watching the sun pop over the horizon at the early church service. Starting with a golden-pink glow to signal it was coming, it slowly, slowly made its journey until suddenly the whole world was aglow. It was astounding to watch it transform the sky as it started its daytime journey over ever-changing terrain. No wonder people always said, "What a difference a day makes." They said it because it was true.

"I should watch the sun come up every day," he said to Big Mike. "I'd get more done."

"I don't know," Big Mike yawned. "I like sleeping in myself."

The big round clock on the auditorium building showed two o'clock in the afternoon. Barely half the day gone and Chico already needed a nap. But that didn't look like it was about to happen any time soon because their whole day was scheduled in half hour increments of fun camp activities. It was going to take some doing to get used to this getting up at sunrise. Maybe he should rethink his early riser plan and choose the evening service instead. He'd talk to Talula about it when he saw her again. The girls were swimming in the "Girl's Only" pool. He knew this because he had found a girl's Xeroxed schedule floating around in the breeze near the cafeteria earlier. As he perused it, he realized their schedule was basically the same as the boys' schedule, but still the church camp counselors insisted on making two schedules so there would be absolutely no confusion.

At least he and Talula hadn't seen any more of Mr. Snakeskin Boots, whose real name someone told them was Arnold Simpson. They also found out he was actually a deacon in the church. The fact that they hadn't noticed him from church already spoke to how few times Chico and Talula went to church. Maybe he should work more church into his new schedule. The sermons would probably be more interesting to him now than when he was a little kid. When he was small, it was all he could do to sit through the service. Pure torture, it was.

Stretching out under a shady tree, Chico observed all the kids walking to the two identical swimming areas. The only difference being the male and female signs hanging at the pool entrances. Oh well, swimming would be fun, girls or no girls. It was time to go get his swimsuit on, but he rested just a moment longer. And, while he basked in the warm sunshine and imbibed the nearby scent of honeysuckle, he thanked God that nothing seemed to be happening as far as anyone coming after him for trespassing in the trailer a few days ago. All in all, he felt peaceful as he got up to go get ready for a dip in the "Boy's Only" pool.

Chico still hadn't told Talula about what really happened when he went back to the trailer. He had

discussed it with Big Mike, though. Talula really didn't
need to know more. She hadn't been with him, and
maybe the two men hadn't seen her that day when they
came over to investigate who was feeding Silver; although
everyone in town knew Talula was the person to call to
feed your animals for you because she took such good
care of them. Mr. Jamison employed her constantly to
care for Silver. He wished she hadn't put out her "Talula
Moonstone's Pet Sitting Service "business cards all over
town. They were bright pink and they had both her
phone number and address on them in bold lettering.

Walking across the lawn and into the boys'
barracks—that wasn't just a name, they were old army
barracks—he realized he was the only one inside.
Tempted to take a nap, he stretched out on his bottom
bunk bed. Before he knew it, he had drifted off into a
light sleep.

At first the tickling feeling annoyed him. Then it
started to really irritate him. That's about the time Chico
opened his eyes and saw a person's arm coming down
from the upper bunk holding a feather. Quickly, he
latched onto the offending arm and gave it a hard tweak.

"Yeow-ouch!" Chico heard Randall yell from the
bunk bed above him. Then he heard a gasp for air as
Randall yelled down again from the upper bunk, "Chico,
you're pretty strong for a stupid person."

He looked longingly at the eagle feather grasped in
Randall's sweaty fist. It would make a nice souvenir from
camp. So, while still holding onto Randall's arm, Chico
used his other hand to attempt to take the feather from
Randall's tightly clenched hand.

But Randall wouldn't let go.

Chico jerked down harder on Randall's arm. A
corresponding scream could be heard from the mattress

above, and Randall immediately let the feather fall from his clutch.

Picking it up, Chico said, "You okay up there?" as he examined his new treasure.

"Yeah, just my luck to be sleeping over you." Randall sounded like he might cry.

Chico felt bad for pulling his arm. "Hey, let's go swim."

"Nah, I don't want to swim." Randall sounded even worse.

"Why not?"

"Because I don't want to wear a swimsuit."

Chico was surprised by this remark. Randall didn't seem like the shy type.

"There's not going to be any girls at our pool. They've segregated us."

"You know, that's an awfully big word for you to be using, Chucklehead."

"Come on, Randall. Get your suit on." Chico didn't take the bait for another argument. He was hot. And he wanted to go swimming. "Wear your shorts if you don't have a swimsuit."

Randall didn't answer. So Chico grabbed his swimsuit and made a quick change. Getting a towel, he started to leave Randall behind, but not before trying one more time.

"Come on, Randall. Get your suit on." As Chico said it, he remembered what Talula had told him about Randall once. She said she felt Randall wanted to be civilized and have friends, he just went about forming friendships backwards. She went on to elaborate that he had a habit of offending people he liked. With this thought in mind, Chico asked him to go swimming one more time.

Randall still didn't answer. And even though Chico couldn't see him in the top bunk, he heard the metal springs as he turned over on his side.

Then just before Chico reached the door, Randall said. "I'm fat."

"What?"

"I'm fat. And I don't want to wear a swimsuit."

Chico stood and contemplated the situation. This was not the Randall he was accustomed to, the Randall he often feared and hid from. In fact, pulling on Randall's arm had been the first time he'd really fought back. To be honest, when he'd first defensively grabbed him, just like he'd learned in Miss Lancer's Aiki lessons, he didn't even know it was Randall. If he had known, there was a good chance he'd have just run out of the barracks and hid. Yet here they were, actually having some kind of conversation over Randall's body image problems.

"Well, why don't you wear a t-shirt with your swimsuit? People do it all the time to keep from getting a sunburn."

"You go ahead. I'll come later. Wouldn't want anyone thinking we were friends."

Chico shook his head before letting the screen door slam behind him. Now he felt bad for calling Randall "Fat Boy," even if it was only in his head most times.

Talula was dog paddling along the side of the girls only pool while Janie sunned herself like a turtle on one of the lounge chairs. When Janie looked her way, Talula motioned for her to come on in. It didn't take a lot of persuasion for Janie to hop down the pool ladder into the cool water as it was a very hot day.

Watching Janie splash water at her with her hands,

Talula couldn't help but be a little envious at how good her new friend looked in her hot pink bikini. *And were those real gold hoop earrings dangling from her pierced ears?* When Talula had asked to get her ears pierced, her mother had just said, "Maybe when you're a little older, dear."

"How's it going?" Janie's voice woke Talula from her reverie.

"So-so," she answered. "I wish Chico and Big Mike could swim with us."

"The boys would just splash us and make lots of noise," Janie said, being careful not to get her face in the water when she dipped her head backwards in the pool to get her hair wet.

"You wear makeup at the pool?" Talula said in wonder as she admired Janie's long polished nails holding on to the pool's edge near her own. Quickly, she tucked her own bitten-down nails under so they weren't visible.

"Yeah, I wear makeup all the time." Janie stopped and looked over at Talula hiding her nails.

"I bet you look good without it, too." Talula said. "You're one of those naturally beautiful types."

"Before I started wearing makeup, I looked awful." Janie confided in a whisper.

"When did you start wearing it?"

"About your age," Janie hesitated before adding, "I bet you'd look good with makeup. Want me to do your face for the evening church service?"

Talula considered this but didn't answer as she wondered if the guys would make fun of her for trying to improve her looks. Finally, she said, "Girly-girl stuff would probably look stupid on me."

"I bet Chico would notice you even more." Janie smiled as she said it.

Talula felt her face go hot. "He doesn't think of me

like that."

"Just let me do your hair then. It'll be fun."

Janie's last request reminded Talula of when she was little and her Mom used to make funny shapes with her hair when she shampooed it. She'd suds it up really high and create funny shapes like rabbit ears.

"Okay, just the hair."

A shrill whistle sounded from the life guard stand. Talula looked up to see Miss Lancer gesturing for them to get out of the water. Quickly, Janie and Talula climbed out of the pool and headed toward their towels. Noticing how Janie took her towel and wrapped it around her waist like a Hawaiian skirt, Talula did the exact same thing.

Freshly showered and ready to be transformed, Talula sat in front of a big mirror in the girls' barracks. Janie was inspecting her with a bit of a frown on her face. Suddenly she announced, "I know just the look for you." Plugging in her hair dryer, she went to work.

The hair dryer got really hot at times and burned the tops of Talula's ears, but she didn't complain. She was ready to sacrifice in order to look like Janie and her beautiful friends.

After a few minutes of lifting long locks of Talula's hair, Janie stopped the dryer. "Your hair's going to take forever to dry."

"Sometimes I stand up and turn over. Then I dry it upside down while I shake my head," Talula said. "It makes it dry a lot faster."

Janie looked at her confused.

"Like this." Talula bent at the waist shaking her long hair out and over her head. She took the hair dryer from Janie's hand and started drying her hair while shaking it back and forth.

Another girl, who was doing her hair nearby, said over the noise, "I do that, too. It dries faster and it adds volume."

Just then Wanda Wright walked in and started putting on her makeup in another mirror on the wall behind them. Even upside down, Talula couldn't help but notice she was watching her.

Finally, Talula turned the dryer off and stood up straight.

"I can't believe your hair's not tangled," Janie said.

"My hair never tangles. It's just kind of slippery straight. I can't get a barrette or anything to stay in . . . it just slides out."

"Here, let me brush it out." Janie started pulling the brush in her hand through Talula's thick hair and, sure enough, it didn't get stuck once, although Talula's head felt like it was going to be tugged off.

Every once in a while Talula looked in the mirror to watch Wanda watching them. She was pretty sure Wanda didn't like her.

Suddenly, Wanda spoke as she applied mascara. "Hey, Janie, you know what you should do..." Her mouth stretched open wide as she continued applying mascara. "You should iron her hair flat."

"Oh yeah, I should," Janie answered. "It'd make it really shiny."

Talula made no comment. She had never had her hair ironed before.

Then before she could answer, the other girl working on her hair beside them pointed to an iron and ironing board. "You can use this one. They have it here so we can touch up the wrinkles in our church clothes."

Pulling Talula in one hand and the chair in the other,

Janie moved toward the iron. "I'll need a fresh towel," she said. Talula allowed herself to be pushed into the chair, her back to the ironing board.

"Here, lean way back," Janie said. "I want to put as much of your hair as I can across the ironing board."

Wanda brought a clean towel to put over her hair. Talula worried Wanda was up to no good.

Janie licked her finger and touched the iron. It hissed. "It's ready," she said.

Wanda brushed Talula's hair over the ironing board, making it as straight as possible. Then she put the thin towel over it. Janie began lightly ironing. Every few seconds Wanda lifted the towel so they could look at their work, all while Talula stayed very still and waited. She really liked her hair and hoped they wouldn't mess it up. Her imagination ran free with images of herself raising up while her hair stayed behind on the ironing board, or starting to brush her hair, and it was so fried from the ironing that it broke off in big chunks. These thoughts were running rampant when Janie stopped ironing and Wanda whipped off the towel.

"Voilà!" Janie cried out as Talula stood up and her hair fell down her back. Looking in the mirror, she could see her super-shiny, super-straight hair reflecting back from the row of mirrors behind them. And she could also see herself looking in the mirror at her hair. Because of the way the two rows of mirrors were positioned she could actually see herself into infinity. She had always liked it when mirrors set up where she could do this sort of thing and, quite honestly, it was hard to pull herself away. So it was something of a relief when Janie moved the chair away from the ironing board and sat her down near the natural sunlight from an open window.

"I'm going to need some good light…" Janie

explained as she pulled up a small towel stand and set her makeup bag on the top.

"Not too much, Janie," Wanda said as she assisted her.

Talula couldn't help but wonder when Wanda said this if she was worried Talula might actually look good. Or, maybe Talula was overreacting to Wanda, maybe she just wanted to help her. After all, she was right: too much makeup on a person who didn't wear makeup might be shocking. Wanda did appear to know a thing or two about beauty. Just one look at her perfect coiffed feathered hair with winged bangs confirmed that.

"Yeah, I know." Janie said as she got down to work. Mixing and blending, she put eye shadow, blush, and mascara on Talula's face. Like Picasso, she took her artwork seriously and only talked to give a few hints here and there on how to make it work when Talula was doing it herself.

Wanda went and got another chair so she could sit nearby and watch the transformation in progress. As other girls came in to the dressing area to get ready for church, they also stopped every so often and watched the proceedings.

Finally the big reveal moment came.

"Close your eyes," Janie said as she led Talula to the mirror. "Now, open them."

Talula heard someone saying, "Oh, Talula. You look great."

And when she opened her eyes she had to agree. A modern miracle had occurred in the girl's church camp locker room that day.

It was hard for Chico to sit still on the hard wooden

pews. Honestly, he liked everything about church camp except for the actual church service part. Or "churchin'," as Big Mike like to call sitting in the services. As in, "You need some more churchin', Chico. Five hours of churchin' is not enough for a kid like you. More churchin' is what you need."

Big Mike also found a multitude of ways to get Chico through the morning, afternoon, and evening sermons; listening was usually not one of them. But rolling jawbreakers down the slightly slanted floor under the pews toward the preacher was. He would lean over as if he dropped something, then he would throw one hard trying to make it all the way to the front without hitting someone's feet. It was truly surprising how often he was able to accomplish this. The few times he hit someone they could never figure out who threw it, and it was funny to watch them look around for the culprit.

So it was that day that Chico and Big Mike found themselves at yet another church service when Talula and Janie walked into the open-air auditorium near where they were sitting. Big Mike saw them first and he dropped his whole box of jawbreakers. They rolled noisily toward the front as everyone looked down under the pews to see what the noise was about. Chico had just started to laugh when Big Mike punched him and pointed toward Talula.

Chico turned to look in the direction Big Mike indicated.

He was overwhelmed.

Talula looked magnificent, much prettier than Janie and any of Janie's other friends. And that was saying a lot.

"Look at her boobs," Big Mike whispered.

"What about them?" Chico said as he continued to stare.

"She has them. I've never noticed them before."

Slowly, Talula and Janie headed toward them and the boys scooted down to make room. But then, for some reason, Chico found himself unable to speak when Talula sat down right beside him. Maybe it was because he didn't know what to say. For instance, would it be a compliment or an insult if he said, "You look great with makeup on. You should wear it everyday." So he decided to say something nebulous like, "You look nice tonight." And he was just about to get this out when Big Mike said, "Talula, you look especially lovely tonight. You should wear your hair like that more often."

He saw Talula's shoulders visibly relax when she realized Big Mike's reaction to her makeover was positive.

Dagnabbit, Big Mike stole the moment.

"Yeah, it looks good. You look good." Chico was embarrassed because his voice was stiff and hoarse with none of the suave sophistication Big Mike had shown.

Someone from behind tapped him on the shoulder. It was Randall. Moving forward he whispered in Chico's ear loud enough for Talula to hear, "Hey, Dumbo, your girlfriend's a lot less ugly looking with makeup on."

Looking straight ahead, Chico tried to ignore him. In fact, he didn't mean to pop Randall when he leaned forward to make another snide remark about Talula, his hand just kind of flew up and found its mark. Chico was as surprised as anybody when bright red blood started spurting from Randall's nose.

One of the camp's counselors quickly pulled out a handkerchief and handed it to Randall before rushing him out the main entrance. The congregation was astir as the counselor maneuvered Randall through the few people still filtering down the aisle to be seated. Chico noted the horror in their faces as they moved aside to let the bloody boy through.

Just as the crowd noise rose in reaction to Randall's predicament, the music started signaling the services were about to begin. The choir sang a song as the last of the people found a seat. After the song, the choir sat back down and the preacher approached the microphone to start his sermon of fire and brimstone brought to you straight from Revelation.

Chico continued to look straight ahead at the pulpit. He was very angry with himself for hurting Randall. *Why did he pop him so hard?* He was having thoughts like this when Talula picked up his hand. Her soft touch soothed him and he began to settle back down.

As the sermon got underway he felt he had to concentrate on something but he couldn't think of anything to think about and Big Mike was out of jawbreakers so he listened to the preacher for once, every single word. And it touched his heart in a way he'd never felt.

He tried not to move his hand that Talula was holding lest she think he wanted her to drop it. So he kept his hand perfectly still except for once when he let go to wipe the sweat that was forming on his palm off on his jeans. Then he grabbed her hand again. He didn't want her to change her mind.

He remembered how when they were younger she had told him she didn't want to grow up and date and stuff. She really just wanted to stay a tomboy forever. But tonight was different. She seemed to be different inside as well as out.

As the preacher asked the congregation to bow their heads to pray, Chico said a silent thank you to God that nothing had happened to them as far as Mr. Snakeskin Boots was concerned. Not taking Talula back with him to check out the trailer had definitely been the right move. If anybody was in trouble it would just be him.

Mr. Snakeskin Boots was sitting a few rows in front of them, nodding off to sleep. Chico noted he didn't look like an evil murderer. He was a deacon after all. Deacons didn't kill people.

CHAPTER 6

Randall had spat chewing gum near where Chico was standing so when he got up to go out on the field he stepped in it. He tried to scrape it off by rubbing his shoe on a wooden railroad tie that was being used to mark off the baseball field from the spectators' area. But because the day was hot, this made more of a problem as the gum stretched in a large blue-green mess. Picking up a stick, he attempted to use it to get the gum off. However, this only resulted in him pulling the sticky mess out into thin ribbons that caught in the air. Looking down he saw quite a bit of it had blown back on him.

"Dang it, Randall," Chico murmured to himself. "These are my new shoes."

"New, huh? I thought those boats used to belong to Big Mike."

"Hey, Chico," the camp counselor yelled in his direction, "get on the field."

Looking back over his shoulder Chico saw the other players waiting for him. Without another thought, he turned and ran on the field with a few thin blue-green threads of gum trailing from his new-to-him shoes. Taking his turn at bat, he tapped home plate three times. He choked up on the bat a little and stuck his butt out as he got into position to swing.

The pitcher threw it. And Chico nailed it.

Looking back as he ran, he could see and hear the crowd going wild.

Big Mike was the catcher and he was motioning him to come on in to home plate.

Just as he heard the word, "Safe," he looked up to see Mr. Snakeskin Boots behind the nearby net. His expression cold in spite of the fact he was clapping wildly.

Getting up, Chico discovered he had made a hole in the seat of his jeans when he slid into safety. Thank God he had new underwear. And, he wasn't swearing; he really did thank God for the new underwear and the new shoes. They were making a difference in his athletic prowess. He thought back to a commercial about tennis shoes that could make you run faster and jump higher. Those shoes looked so great and he'd always wanted them, but his mother could never afford them so he didn't even ask. "Well, mister," he thought to himself, "you got yourself some pretty special shoes now. Like superhuman running shoes."

As Randall came up to bat, he held out his hand to Chico in a surprisingly genuine gesture of team spirit. But as he shook hands, he said these not-so-surprising words under his breath, "Way to go, Chucklehead."

On the bench, Chico watched Randall strike out. Then, gritting his teeth into more of a grimace than a smile, he used a rock to scrape the rest of the gum off his sole.

Looking nice took a lot of time, as Talula was discovering. You had to wake up early to do your hair and makeup, and you actually had to think about what you were going to wear. Then after you put it on, you had to check yourself in the mirror occasionally.

Right now, the girls were getting ready to go to the pool, and even though there were no guys in the girl's pool, Janie and all her friends wore makeup. So, Talula borrowed a little of this and that from the different girls lined up in front of the mirrors. In truth, they were all too happy to make suggestions and share. This made Talula think maybe she was really bad off to start with and they knew every little bit of makeup would help. However, she guessed it was the same for most of the girls because everyone looked better wearing it.

Later, out in the pool, Talula felt like her freshly applied face was melting. Apparently, the mascara she had borrowed today was not waterproof. It was running and making a mess.

"Are you crying?" Janie asked when she saw Talula wiping her eyes on the corner of her beach towel.

"Sort of, my mascara's running. It's burning my eyes."

"Oh, yeah. It does that. Just don't rub it, you'll make it worse."

"I think I need to go back to the girls' barracks and wash it off."

"Do you want me to go with you?"

"No, I'm not that bad off. I can still see."

Talula turned to go, but before she got to the pool gate, Janie called out, "Hey, Talula. You can use my waterproof mascara. My makeup bag is on top of my suitcase."

"No, I'll just go without for the rest of the day."

"You can't go without makeup now that you've started wearing makeup."

"Why not?"

"People will expect you to look a certain way now. They'll notice."

Talula had a sinking feeling in her stomach as she walked back to the girls' barracks, she wasn't sure about all this growing up stuff. Maybe she shouldn't have started the makeup thing if you can't quit it. She wondered what would happen if she showed up at the church service tonight without any mascara. Visions of people gasping in horror filled her mind and she tried to think back if she'd ever noticed if someone who wore makeup suddenly went without it.

Walking back wasn't that easy with her profusely watering eyes. The thought occurred to her she might be allergic to this particular mascara. She could hardly see when she bumped into Chico.

"What's wrong?" Talula recognized Chico's voice.

Without a word, she pulled the beach towel away from her face and wrapped it around her waist as she'd seen Janie do earlier. "I'm allergic to this mascara I borrowed. I'm going to the girls' barracks to wash it off."

"Here, I'll guide you." He gently took her arm as if she were really blind and started to give her verbal instructions. "We're approaching three steps down. Careful, there's a big crack in the sidewalk."

Talula moved forward, cautiously putting one foot in front of the other. It never ceased to amaze her how Chico appeared just when she needed him most.

"Why aren't you at the boys' pool?" Talula asked as she held on tight to his arm.

"Oh, I don't know. Thought I'd go back and take a nap."

"Are we almost there?"

"Yes, just a little bit farther. Do you need me to lead you inside?"

"Just get me to the sink. I don't want you to get in trouble."

Talula held her hands out as Chico gently maneuvered to a line of sinks in the girls' locker room. Once there, Talula felt about for the cold water handle and twisted it on. She only let it run over her fingers for a few seconds before cupping up the water and splashing it over her eyes. She flooded her stinging eyes with cool water like this for quite some time. Then suddenly she stopped.

Backing away from the running water, she shook off the beach towel she'd wrapped around her waist earlier and held a clean corner to her eyes. "Ahh," she said. "Ahh. Relief."

Her face was still buried in the towel when she felt Chico step forward to turn off the water that was still running full blast.

"This is kind of weird being where girls shower," he said.

"What's so weird about it? "

"I mean, it's weird . . . girls run around without clothes on in this place."

"There are no girls without clothes on in here." Talula's voice held more than a hint of irritation. "There's no one in here but us."

"How are your eyes?"

She felt him pulling the towel away from her face.

"Oh, no," he said. "They're swollen almost shut."

Talula looked into the fluorescent-lit mirror. Her eyes looked like they had been punched.

"Do you think we should go see the nurse?" She

heard the concern in his voice.

"Give me a few minutes. Let's see if they're going to get better or worse now that I've washed all the mascara off."

"Why don't we stretch out on your bunk while we wait? All this getting up early for services is killing me in the afternoons. I can hardly hold my eyes open."

Talula's stomach tightened. Even though he did look exhausted, she knew he wasn't supposed to be in the girls' barracks.

"I don't know," she said. "We'd get in a lot of trouble if they . . ."

"Come'on . . . we won't even talk. No one will ever know we're in here. We'll just give your eyes a chance to recover."

"I have a bad feeling…"

"You are always having bad feelings and most of the time nothing ever happens. Here," he said as he pulled her to the lower bunk, "is this one yours? Your suitcase is on it, so I guess it's yours."

"Will you reach in and get me a t-shirt and shorts to put over my swimsuit?" Talula motioned to her suitcase. "Even though I've almost dried, I'm still cold."

"Do you want the pink shirt or the yellow one?" he said holding both shirts up to a pair of jean shorts. "Or do you want the tie-dyed one?"

He always rambled when he was trying to get her to do something she thought they shouldn't being doing. The strange part was his voice actually soothed her and calmed her down so that she forgot why it was a bad idea to do what Chico wanted to do. And so she just reached out and grabbed the nearest t-shirt and shorts from his hand.

She shook them out and gave them a quick once

over for spiders or any of the other bugs that seemed to run rampant in the girls' barracks. Then she slipped them on over her almost dry swimsuit before getting into the lower bunkbed that had been assigned to her.

She watched as Chico sat on the side of the bunkbed and took his shoes off before stretching out beside her. The shoes still had traces of gooey gum on the bottom.

"Do you think I look a lot better with makeup?" Talula said, looking across the pillow at him.

"I like you either way," he yawned.

"That's no answer."

Talula felt a small chill run over her as Chico reached out and touched her face. She was so happy to have him to herself like she did at home. No Wanda. No Big Mike. Just the two of them was her favorite thing.

"Hey, I've got to tell you something," he said seriously.

"About Mr. Snakeskin Boots?"

"No, about Jesus Christ."

Now, this wasn't an answer Talula expected; Chico never said much about anything spiritual. In fact, she wasn't really sure where he stood on the issue.

She looked into his eyes as he continued. "I got saved yesterday at the church service."

"Oh, Chico," She reached out and hugged him. "That's the best news ever!"

As she pulled back, he kept his arm wrapped around her shoulders. "Yeah, it surprised even me. But I knew. I just knew God was there and he sent Jesus to save us. I knew it was true."

"Do you feel different? I didn't really feel too much different when I got saved, but I *was* different, if you know what I mean."

"Yeah, everything I was hearing just rang true."

Chico's voice was soft and low, not just because he didn't want anyone to hear them talking, but because he was drifting off to sleep.

"Funny how some of the biggest moments in your life are also the most common," Talula said softly, although she was fairly certain he didn't hear her as his breathing was becoming almost a snore. Getting up early for church service certainly did make Chico sleepy in the afternoons. He wasn't really what you'd call a morning person.

Looking at the bottom of the bunk overhead, she pulled at a string that was hanging down from the mattress, then she settled down into Chico's arms. Talula knew this would be a moment she would think about a lot in the future, so she tried to memorize it: how the air felt hot and humid in spite of the fact ceiling fans and large floor fans worked overtime, how the barracks smelled like baby powder and perfume mixed with some strange mildewy odor. Looking around, she saw half-unpacked suitcases with lots of clothes hanging from every available space making for a crazy, colorful, carnival type atmosphere.

She felt Chico moving his arm behind her, trying to get as comfortable as he could without taking his arm away. Positioning her head on his chest, she rearranged her body so he could move freely, and when she looked up at his face, she noticed his eyes were still closed.

Moving her head over his chest, she found the spot where she was able to listen to his heart. It drummed slow and steady. A gentle breeze blew over them in tiny puffs through the screened-in window. Her eyes didn't hurt at all now. Everything was perfect. "I can't fall asleep too, or we'll get caught for certain," she thought as her eyelids grew heavy.

At first the cold feel of metal at his temple felt good. After all, the big fans weren't really doing their job in the humid summer heat. But then the cold metal object began to push too hard. In a dreamlike state, Chico swatted at his forehead. In the next instant someone reached out and shook him really hard. Now fully awake, he recognized the scowling face of Arnold Simpson, a.k.a. Mr. Snakeskin Boots, hovering over him, holding a gun. Instinctively, Chico knew not to yell. He hoped if he didn't wake Talula, Arnold Simpson would leave her alone.

"Wake the girl and get her suitcase," Arnold said in a low, gruff whisper.

"At least he's not going to kill us if he wants me to bring her suitcase," Chico thought as he tucked Talula's old case up under his arm. It wasn't very large and it didn't have much in it. Reaching down beside the bed, he also picked up his new sneakers that he got from Big Mike's mom. He'd kicked them off when they'd decided to lay down.

Arnold waved the gun in Talula's direction, indicating he wanted her to come as well. Chico gently shook Talula. Slowly, she opened her still swollen eyes and gasped. Chico was surprised she'd slept this long. Usually Talula would wake up at the slightest noise. Or, at least, that's what she'd told him; he hadn't really actually slept anywhere near her until today.

"Now, you're both going to walk out with me and get in my car," Arnold said directly into Chico's face. Chico couldn't help but notice his smoker's breath—stale, stinky, like a walking ashtray. Thank goodness Arnold had breathed in his face instead of Talula's because she'd cough and have trouble breathing. Smoker's breath was hard for her to take; it made her asthma act up. But Chico knew crazy thoughts like these weren't going to save them. He needed to distract Arnold Simpson and get him away from Talula.

"Can I pee first?" Chico motioned his head toward the girl's bathroom with its long line of stalls.

"No, you cannot pee." Arnold Simpson shoved Chico out the barracks door.

Roughly, Arnold Simpson pushed Chico and Talula along the path to the parking lot. In the distance, Chico saw Big Mike headed toward them. He was waving.

"Hey, aren't you going swimming?" Big Mike yelled.

"No," Arnold Simpson answered back. "He needs to go home. His father is sick."

Chico knew this must have taken Big Mike by surprise, as his father hadn't contacted the family since he left. He watched as Big Mike kept coming toward them with a questioning look on his face. Arnold Simpson looked irritated. Chico felt him punch the gun harder into his back and his grip tightened on his arm.

When Big Mike reached them, he wasted no time getting right up in Arnold Simpson's face as he said, "Well, that's kind of weird considering no one's heard from his father for over a year." Before the words registered with Arnold Simpson, Big Mike clocked him in the nose with his left hand while grabbing the gun he was holding with his right.

The gun went off.

Arnold Simpson fell back on the hard ground, not because he'd been shot, but because Big Mike had knocked him out cold. The boys and Talula whirled around. The stray bullet had lodged in the trunk of a tree.

Chico bent down and got the car keys from Arnold

Simpson's pocket. Raw fear made all three of them run as they jumped into Arnold Simpson's nearby car.

Chico swung Talula's suitcase in the backseat and moved in behind the steering wheel. It took him a moment he couldn't spare to figure out the dashboard. As he turned the key, country music started to blare from the radio. Arnold Simpson started to stir on the ground. Big Mike punched the radio off while Chico slowly backed the car out of its parking space. He turned and looked out the back window to make certain he wouldn't hit anyone.

"Talula. Where's Talula?" Panic filled his voice.

"I'm down here in the backseat floorboard." She was using that stilted non-emotional voice she'd used at Silver's feed shed the day they heard the shots. He knew she was trying to cover her fear.

"Stay down."

His heart drummed in his ears as he popped the car into gear and took off. Looking down, Chico noticed Big Mike still had the gun in his hand.

"What should I do with it?" Big Mike said.

"I don't know."

"*You don't know?*" Big Mike's voice indicated he was starting to go a little crazy.

"Here," Chico leaned over and pulled open the glove compartment. The car swerved and he immediately overcorrected. His sister had been teaching him to drive, but they'd only had a few lessons. He'd better slow it down if he didn't want to wreck.

When the car was stable again, Big Mike regained his composure, too. He carefully positioned the gun in the compartment by pointing it away from them before securely shutting it back.

From the back, Chico heard Talula's tiny voice say, "What's happening? What are we going to do now?"

"We're going to the boys' barracks and we're going to get our stuff," Chico said.

"Then what are we going to do?" Talula asked.

"We're going to get as far away from here as possible."

"Then what?" And he wanted to answer her, but he didn't have an answer.

CHAPTER 7

Chico kept looking back over his shoulder, his hands shaking hard as he tried to throw his stuff into his beat up suitcase. He noted Big Mike was already zipping his case shut, and he wondered if Talula was doing okay. They'd left her and her suitcase down in the floorboard of the back seat while they got their things. No one had formed a plan yet, but it seemed obvious church camp wasn't going to be the safe haven they first thought.

"Let's go," Chico said to Big Mike as he stuffed the last shirt in and started to zip.

Running out the front door, they encountered Randall coming inside. "What's up?" Randall asked just as the sound of tires squealing made all three boys turn and look.

Chico pushed Randall aside and started running in the direction of the car. It looked to him as if Arnold were the driver and the rest of the car was empty, but then Chico died a little bit inside as he saw Talula rise up in the back seat with duct tape across her mouth. Arnold Simpson must have seen her in the rearview because he pushed her body back down without ever taking his eyes off the road.

Big Mike yelled out to Chico, "Over here! Randall is old enough to drive and he has access to a church van."

Chico turned to see Big Mike and Randall getting into a white van with a Hilltop Church logo on its side. As Chico reached the open sliding passenger door, he heard Randall start the engine. Quickly, he threw his suitcase in the back and slammed the big doors shut. Randall pulled out to follow Arnold before Chico even had a chance to get seated.

"Don't race. I don't want them to know we're following them," Chico yelled at Randall as he fell onto the van's hard passenger bench in back.

"Okay, okay. Don't get your tail in a twist. But we might lose them," Randall cautioned.

"No, there's only one main road out of this camp." Chico rubbed his left hand. He'd fallen on it wrong after he shut the door. It hurt bad, but he didn't mention it. Instead, he asked Randall how he'd gotten access to the van.

"Oh, I used it the other day to go get ice cream in town," Randall said matter-of-factly as if they let all the campers use the van. "They leave the key in it," he continued. "So I guess it's okay for us to take it, right? If they didn't want us using it, they wouldn't leave the key in it."

Chico didn't even try to make sense of Randall's reasoning, instead he changed the subject. "Did you see the duct tape on Talula's mouth?"

"Yeah," both Randall and Big Mike answered at once.

"Now, when they get to the highway up ahead, you can start to tail them a little closer." Chico's voice was calm and steady. "Wouldn't want to lose them at this point."

"You know, you two should get down so he won't see you in the rearview," Randall said. Big Mike scrambled in between the driver's seat and the passenger bench seat, maneuvering his way to the back. There he stretched out flat on the carpeted floorboard, pushing Chico up against the very back of the van, a position that Chico didn't exactly favor, but it was what it was. Randall had made a valid point. They needed to stay out of sight.

"Hey, Randall," Chico hesitated. "Thanks for helping us."

"You're welcome, twerp." Randall said as he purposely swerved the van jerking Big Mike so he'd roll to the back squishing Chico.

Raising her head, Talula looked through the back window long enough to see Chico, Big Mike, and Randall running toward Arnold's car, but she didn't hold out much hope they'd be able to help her. She thought about raising her head again to see which direction they were going, but judging by the way Snakeskin (in her mind, she'd shortened his name to just one descriptive word) had shoved her back down, she dared not do it very often. In a minute, she would try again.

Right now, she turned her attention to loosening the ties on her hands. He'd tied her hands with shoelaces, and if she pulled really, *really* hard they stretched a bit, almost enough for her to get a hand out.

One thing was for sure: she was going to have to keep thinking if she was going to get away. She was proud of herself for having the clarity of mind to ask Snakeskin why he was trying to kidnap them before he duct taped her mouth shut. He had muttered his answer so low she could barely hear him. "Because you two heard us get in a fight with the man at the trailer over his horse. You heard the shots. He was wounded, and I want to know what happened to him. Where is he? We know your friend went back to the trailer that night."

"You shot a man?" she stammered. "I thought it was firecrackers. Chico went back and looked, and he said it was firecrackers..." was all she'd been able to get out before he'd angrily slapped the duct tape over her mouth. Asthma and a ducted-taped mouth weren't a great combo, and it was really hard to breathe through her nose. She thought she was going to pass out. But instead she forced herself to sit up, just for a moment, long enough to see they were coming up on the Dairy Royal they'd eaten at on the way to camp. Snakeskin was headed back the way they came.

Twisting and pulling, she stretched the shoelaces so they no longer bound her hands tight. As she worked she thought about napping with Chico earlier. It had been one of the happiest moments of her life, and she didn't much believe in happiness, what with the way her parents fought. They screamed and yelled so often it had given her the start of an ulcer when she was only five. Her grandparents fought, too. Therefore, Talula had decided she would never fall in love. Love led to misery from her point of view. Her position on love was usually curled up in a fetal position in bed late at night while her parents battled it out, screaming ugly, hateful things they'd forget in the morning, but she never would. The shoe laces were loosening on her right hand.

"Think pleasant thoughts," she reminded herself. Thinking about parental ineptitudes would only make her asthma worse, so she returned to thoughts of Chico. He made her happy, but she was afraid to get too close as he might reject her, and it would ruin their friendship. In the past, she usually tried to reject him first, just in case he was going to reject her.

Twisting and pulling she wrenched one hand free. "Man, it really, really hurt. Dagnabbit," she couldn't help thinking. She knew Chico would be mad about her cussing even if it was in her head. So she didn't.

The car was slowing down to turn. She popped her head up for another quick look. Sure enough, it was the same Dairy Royal they'd eaten at on the way to camp. Unbelievable, Snakeskin was stopping at the Dairy Royal. "I guess kidnappers have to eat, too," she thought. Slipping her hand back into the laces, she rolled over and looked up. He was pulling into a space on the empty side of the restaurant where no one would notice a bound-up kid in the backseat. Stopping the car, he thoughtfully rolled down the windows. "Wouldn't want the Texas heat to kill the kidnap victim," Talula thought.

"Stay put," Snakeskin snarled as he stepped out of the car. She heard his footsteps crunching gravel as he headed inside.

Working fast, Talula slipped her hand back out of the laces and ripped the duct tape off her mouth. For a moment she contemplated running into the Dairy Royal for help, but Snakeskin was the kind of man who'd hurt someone who got in his way. He might have another gun or a knife on him. So she went with her plan number two: grab her little suitcase and run like hell. "Sorry about the cussing, Chico. I know it isn't attractive," she thought, if only Chico were here to hear her.

Once she was out of the car, she ran down an alley into a neighborhood. Frantically, she looked back over her shoulder. Through the big plate glass window, she could see Snakeskin standing at the Dairy Royal counter with his back to her. Without a second thought, Talula threw the suitcase into a clump of bushes. Then she jumped up on a nearby wooden fence and began to climb. It wasn't that hard since it had a cross timber about three feet up. With this foothold, she was able to hoist herself on over the top of the fence. Now, coming down on the other side was a different story. There was nothing to hang on to and she fell flat on her back onto someone's freshly mowed lawn. It was sort of soft, but not really.

She lay there, trying to catch her breath. Lying flat out on her back, looking up at the sun, Talula was thinking about her next move when a giant mastiff walked up and let his slobber dribble down over her forehead. Without a doubt, it'd been a while since the big dog had a bath. She almost passed out from the smell. When she brought her hand to her face to try to pinch her nose shut, he moved to her right side and began to lick her face. At least he liked her. She shivered to think what might have happened if he had disliked her even a little bit.

She pulled at the tag on his worn leather collar. Engraved on one side of the dirty silver medallion was the name "Bullwinkle" and an address.

Now, Bullwinkle was big and mean-looking. That's why his owner had purchased him as a guard dog—to protect his family and property against intruders. But Bullwinkle only looked bad, he was really quite gentle and loving. The only problem was not too many people wanted to get close enough to him to love him back. Perhaps it was because he only got a bath twice a year and, it was true, he had acquired the peculiar habit of eating his own poop. But that was definitely not a subject Bullwinkle would have discussed with Talula, even if he could talk like a human, because it embarrassed him that his owner made such a big deal out of it. Yelling. Screaming. Making gagging noises. Didn't the guy know poop tasted great?

Besides, this girl didn't seem to mind his doggie breath and slobbery kisses. In fact, she gave him a nice rub on his left ear after he licked her cheek. As he nudged her with his nose, Bullwinkle decided she must be an angel. A true angel sent down from heaven. And she had chosen to fall in his backyard.

These were the kinds of thoughts Bullwinkle was having upon Talula's imminent arrival in his territory, only Talula would never know because of the dog/human language barrier. But one thing was clear to them both: they were happy to make each other's acquaintance.

Chico noticed Big Mike was curled up in a most uncomfortable-looking position on the carpeted floorboard. Thank goodness he wasn't as tall as Big Mike because he could stay a bit more unfurled. Still, he could not find a comfortable position.

"Hey, they're turning into the Dairy Royal we ate at on the way out here." Randall started slowing down and he heard the turn signal starting to click.

"Don't let him see you," Chico hissed. "Park far away from him."

"Okay, I'll park on this side and watch my rearview," Randall's voice lowered conspiratorially as he gave a play-by-play of Mr. Snakeskin Boots actions. "He's rolling down the windows of the car . . . He's saying something through the window to Talula in the backseat . . . Now he's stepped in gum and he's walking on inside while trying to get it off."

Chico interjected with a hint of sarcasm. "Probably gum you spit out on the way up here."

"Probably so," Randall continued in his animated, whispering announcer voice. "I remember thinking if I spit this gum right here, Talula's kidnapper will walk through it two days from now."

"Quit farting around, Randall." Big Mike's tone had serious implications that he'd kick someone's butt if they messed up this opportunity to get Talula back.

"Hey," Randall interrupted Big Mike, "Talula just jumped out of the car and ran down the alley into a nearby neighborhood."

With that, Randall threw the church van into reverse and backed out to follow her. Popping the gear back into drive, he swung a hard left toward the neighborhood. Chico was rolling about in the back, thankfully mostly on top of Big Mike instead of under him.

Trying to raise his head to look out the window, Chico jumped out of his skin when Randall yelled in alarm, "She's going over a wooden fence!"

Chico tried to stay calm. "Pull up to it. I'll get out and follow her."

"No," Randall said, glancing in the rearview. Chico didn't have to ask, he knew Randall saw Mr. Snakeskin coming back to his car. In seconds, he too would be looking for Talula. Lifting his head, Chico looked out the back window in time to see him questioning an older couple.

"Oh, no. They're pointing in the direction Talula ran," Randall squeaked excitedly.

Chico brought his fist down on the seat. "I should go after her. It doesn't matter if he sees me. You two could meet up with us somewhere."

"Okay, he's getting in his car." Randall was watching in the rearview. "If you're going to get out, do it now." He tapped the brakes and came to a very short stop.

Chico opened the van door and flung himself out and into some overgrown shrubbery. As he did so, he heard Randall asking Big Mike why in the world someone would kidnap Talula.

Watching the big white church van drive away, he worried about Randall knowing what had happened at the trailer. Why had he told Big Mike the whole story that night when he was trying to get him to go with him to the trailer to check things out? The more people involved, the more people might get hurt.

Just then, Arnold Simpson's car rounded the corner and started up the alley. Holding his breath, he prayed for the car to pass by the shrubbery where he was hidden from view. He let out a sigh of relief as it drove by him without slowing down. Once the coast was clear, he looked up at all the fences. Three of them were wooden. He chose the one with the lowest crossbar. And, of course, he chose wrong.

Bullwinkle followed Talula to the front gate wagging his tail, but he kept putting his body in front of hers when she reached for the latch. Trying to push him back so she could get out first was not an option. Each time she opened the gate a little, Bullwinkle pushed his big square nose through. Finally he pushed hard enough to get past her and the gate. Smiling, he turned around and waited for her to follow him out into the house's front yard.

"Heavens to Murgatroyd, Bullwinkle. You get back in this gate."

Bullwinkle proceeded to run around the front yard. Talula figured if she went back into the yard, he'd come back inside. And he did come back to the gate, but every time she approached him, he lopped back to the front yard. If Talula could have read his doggie mind, she'd have known he was thinking, "This is fun. I can do this all day." And, although she wasn't a dog psychic, she did eventually figure this out. So she finally came into the front yard and let him follow her. They'd only gone up the sidewalk a bit when who did they meet but Snakeskin coming down the street in his car.

Suffice it to say, Talula and Bullwinkle ran back in the gate and slammed it shut. Unable to climb the finished side of the fence, she glanced around for a place to hide. Bullwinkle's house seemed like a good choice to her, until Bullwinkle followed in behind her. His massive body squished her petite self up against the back wall as Bullwinkle turned to face their enemy.

She heard the ominous creak of the gate opening and slamming shut. Then Bullwinkle let out a threatening growl. Behind the dog's tall legs, she watched once again as those one-of-a-kind snakeskin boots approached with the intention of doing her harm.

"I'm not afraid of you, dog." Snakeskin bent down and held out a hamburger under the dog's nose long enough for him to get a good whiff. Then he tossed it into the center of the yard.

To Bullwinkle's credit, he did hesitate a moment before leaping after it. Then it only took a second for Snakeskin to reach inside the doghouse and wrench her out by the arm. Quickly, he ushered her past Bullwinkle as he ate the last of the burger. Snakeskin had barely dragged her through the gate when Bullwinkle looked up and lunged for him. Snakeskin had to push hard to make the old latch lock back into place. Behind the rickety fence, Bullwinkle howled in rage.

"Dumb dog," Snakeskin laughed.

In desperation, Talula glanced around to see if anyone in the neighborhood was out on this hot summer day. Not a soul out getting mail or watering a lawn, and obviously Bullwinkle's owners weren't home.

"What are you looking for?" Snakeskin said as he pushed her toward the back seat of his car. "No one is going to rescue you, so you just as well be quiet while I tape you back up."

Talula started to scream. This made Bullwinkle double his efforts to get out. She heard the dog throwing his large bulk against the sagging wooden fence over and over again as Snakeskin pushed her down in the back seat. He held her down with one knee while he tore a strip of duct tape off with his free hand. Reaching under the seat, he pulled out a knife to cut it when he stopped and got a strange look on his face. Slowly he moved back out of the car as he put his hands up in the air. The only sound was Bullwinkle's barking in the background. Raising up, Talula could see Bullwinkle's head and shoulders above the fence line. "Smart dog," she thought. Bullwinkle was standing on top of his house. With just one jump, he'd be over the fence.

As Snakeskin backed away from the car, Talula saw that it wasn't Bullwinkle that Snakeskin feared, it was Chico. Yes, indeed, Chico had come to save her, and he was holding a gun on Snakeskin, the same gun Snakeskin had held on him earlier. Her mind flew as she remembered Big Mike putting it back in the front seat's glove compartment.

As Talula emerged from the car, Snakeskin made a grab for her. He was still holding the knife he'd used to cut the duct tape. "You ain't gonna shoot me, kid," he said as he held the knife against Talula's neck. "You ain't the murdering type," he said, pushing Talula toward the back seat.

She resisted his efforts to put her back in the car by kicking him hard.

"Get in the car, girl!" Snakeskin snarled.

"Don't hurt her," Chico said as he pointed the gun downward. "She didn't see anything."

Suddenly, Snakeskin dropped his knife and his hold on her. Talula looked up in time to see Bullwinkle flying over the fence in a mad furor. Snakeskin jumped in the driver's seat and tried to roll up the window, but Bullwinkle was too fast. Lifting up his hands to protect his face, he let out a loud scream as Bullwinkle's teeth pierced the skin of his upper arm.

Talula took Chico's hand and they started to run. Bullwinkle looked up at them once before attacking Snakeskin's arm again. They heard the engine roar to life as they turned and ran between two houses and hid between two air conditioner units.

Sitting on a concrete slab with their backs up against a brick wall, Talula reached up and ripped duct tape off her mouth for the second time that day. It hurt so bad she wanted to scream, but she didn't. She held her hand over her mouth until Chico gently pulled it away. Looking at her swollen lips, he held her face near his. Slowly his gaze moved up from her lips to her eyes. Talula's heart pounded. Her chest felt tight. It was difficult for her to take more than shallow breaths. And she didn't know if it was from being chased by Snakeskin or from being rescued by Chico.

CHAPTER 8

He wished he were more of a take-charge personality. Talula seemed to be more in control of this situation than him. Looking at her, he wondered if he could ever be the man she wanted him to be. He certainly wasn't the smartest. He didn't even know how to use the gun he'd gotten out of the glove compartment. What if Snakeskin had taken it away from him? Or worse yet, what if he'd accidentally shot himself or Talula?

Talula whispered. "You were great back there."

Her ability to hone in on what was bothering him was incredible.

"But it was the big dog that saved you." Chico's voice was despondent.

"Bullwinkle!" Talula exclaimed.

"Are you trying not to cuss by saying Bullwinkle instead of Bull . . ."

"No, Bullwinkle is the dog's name."

He smothered a chuckle before reaching out to stroke a stray strand of hair near Talula's face. "Okay, how do you know his name? Did you make it up?"

"No, he told me."

Chico laughed again. He could smell the fruity shampoo she had been using lately. Inhaling deeply, he moved in to kiss her. Their lips were almost touching when she whispered. "His name was on his tag."

"Whose name?" Chico was lost in the moment.

"Bullwinkle's."

Suddenly Chico began to laugh and the moment was gone.

"Bullwinkle. Bullwinkle. Bullwinkle." Talula giggled.

Chico laughed at Talula's little Bullwinkle tirade. But only for a moment before the big dog showed up himself.

"Oh, my gosh!" Chico heard Talula say as the giant pooch pushed his way in to their small hiding place. "Bullwinkle, we have to put you back in your yard."

"Or take him with us," Chico reasoned. "I don't think we're going to be able to just pick up the phone and call our parents to come get us. It's obvious Mr. Snakeskin and friends don't want us talking about what we saw, even though we didn't really see anything."

"I need to tell you something," Talula said.

"What?" Chico looked at her as she rubbed Bullwinkle's ear.

"When Snakeskin had me tied up—before he put the duct tape over my mouth—I asked him why they were trying to hurt us and he said it was because we saw them shoot someone."

Chico gazed at her intently before saying, "I lied to you, Talula. It wasn't firecrackers. They're trying to hurt us because we did hear them shoot someone. A man—a man I later found in the woods when I went back."

Talula gasped in shock. "They murdered him and left his body in the woods."

Chico continued. "No, he's alive. I found him in the

woods and helped him into town where we ran into Miss Lancer running, of all things, running in the alley at night." He stopped to let it all sink into Talula's brain.

"It gets weirder," he continued. "Miss Lancer and the gunshot victim knew each other. And Miss Lancer asked me to get Brother Lowe to come to her house to help us with the man's wound, and Brother Lowe knows them both. They didn't take the guy to the hospital or anything. Doctored him right there."

"Brother Lowe was a doctor in the army."

"Talula, you don't *not* take someone that's been shot to the hospital even if you are a doctor."

Talula changed the subject abruptly by asking, "Why do you think Silver is important to them?"

"What does Silver have to do with this?" Chico asked.

"Snakeskin said they shot the man over a horse. I assumed it was Silver."

This news took Chico by complete surprise. For some reason, he assumed it was drug-related or possibly a game of cards gone bad.

"Silver. Why would anyone fight over Silver?"

"Mr. Jamison would. He's so careful with him. I can't believe he doesn't have Silver in a real barn or stable with other horses."

"That's it. Mr. Jamison doesn't board Silver at the stables."

"He has the shed and carport," Talula defended Mr. Jamison.

"It's almost like he's hiding Silver by never mixing him with anyone who has horses."

"That's just crazy talk."

"No, Talula. Silver is special. Why else would they shoot someone over a horse?"

Chico watched Talula rub Bullwinkle's head. She looked like she was about to cry. He felt so bad for lying to her.

"We need to get up and get moving," he said as he stood up and brushed off his jeans.

"I want to go home," she said as he reached down and pulled her hand.

"Okay, but first we're going to make certain we know what's really going on so we can tell the police."

"Why not just tell our parents?" He knew Talula was being reasonable, but it was too dangerous.

"Our parents can't protect us from these two men. I'm not even sure the police can. Heck, for all we know the police might be in on it. I've seen Mr. Snakeskin hanging out with a couple of policemen in town before. They were just having coffee and shooting the breeze, but . . ."

She was staring at him in surprise. "But everyone in our town knows everyone. It doesn't mean the police are in cahoots with Snakeskin. It just means that they've known each other their whole lives."

"Yes, you're right," Chico said as he held out his hand to Talula in an effort to pull her up from her sitting position. "I think it is time to get the police involved, if for no other reason than Snakeskin kidnapped you and duct-taped your mouth shut. Before, we had nothing to tell the police, just that we heard a man get shot and then that same man wouldn't go to the hospital."

"Yes, they'd probably think we were making the story up," Talula said.

He grabbed her hand and gently began to pull her up. "Come on, let's go."

"Where are we going?"

"When I know, I'll tell you. Maybe we can find

Randall and Big Mike driving around in the church van. They must be looking for us."

Here she was in a life or death situation, walking along a sidewalk in a town she wasn't sure the name of, with Chico and a dog named Bullwinkle. If you had told her last week this was to be the case, she'd have flipped out. She looked over at Chico walking briskly beside her, his head bent in thought.

Suddenly, he turned to her and said, "I have money."

You have money?" Talula said incredulously. Then she realized how she sounded, and she softened it by saying, "Oh, thank goodness. I don't have a dime on me."

"I have twenty dollars. My mom gave it to me for emergencies."

"Obviously, this would qualify as an emergency."

She became silent as Chico drew back into his thoughts. After a bit, he turned to her again and said, "I also have the gun."

"What gun?"

"Arnold Simpson's gun. You know, Snakeskin."

Talula stopped walking, forcing Chico and Bullwinkle to do the same. Bullwinkle came to her side and waited expectantly.

"Get rid of it. It's probably the gun they used at the trailer."

"That's exactly why I kept it. Trying not to touch it too much."

"Where is it?"

"Here," Chico pointed to his back as he turned around. She looked at the gun stuck in the back of his pants.

"Careful, you might accidentally shoot yourself in the

behind."

"No, I've got the safety on."

They started walking again, neither saying a word. They walked along this way for some time. At one point Chico reached out and took Talula's hand. And even though it would have been easier not to hold hands at some points along the way, she was careful not to let go, because Talula believed that love isn't always easy and you should always try to hang on to it when you can.

His heart was pounding erratically as a plan was forming in the back of his mind. He recognized this town, or at least this particular area from when he was a boy; his grandfather on his father's side lived in this neighborhood. He'd died just before his dad left them.

Without telling Talula why, he steered her down a street toward his grandfather's old house. He didn't feel like telling her what he was doing because if he did, he might have to talk about what his life was like before his dad left, and that'd make him feel worse than he already did. Instead, he changed the subject by asking her, "How are you feeling?"

"My lips hurt from the duct tape." Her voice was flat and without emotion.

He stopped and turned her toward him. "Let me see." Carefully, he examined her face.

"They're puffy," he said, gently touching her lips with his finger.

"I think I was allergic to the sticky stuff on the tape."

"We could get some medicine to put on them. There's a store near here."

"No, I don't want to spend any of our money on medicine. They'll get better."

Chico let his hands fall from her face to either side of her arms. Looking directly into her eyes, he softly said, "Okay."

Neither moved except for his gentle caressing of her upper arms.

"You're so soft," his voice deepened just a little.

Both were startled when the front door of a house behind them opened and a little gray-haired lady came out with her poodle on a leash. She was carrying a rolled up newspaper and an umbrella even though there was no sign of rain. Giving them a suspicious look, she headed down her front walk with a confident air.

Instinctively, they knew it was best to move on. Both of them looked around for Bullwinkle. He was two houses behind them, sniffing a bush. When they started to walk, he ran toward them, giving the poodle a little fright. The woman tugged the poodle to her side as she fell in step behind them. She gave Bullwinkle a look that said, "Don't mess with me or my dog."

"Boy, she walks fast for an old lady," Chico thought as he pulled Bullwinkle by the collar off the sidewalk and over to the grass. In a moment, the woman and her poodle overtook and passed them. All three of them stood and watched as the lady and her poodle moved on down the street.

"You know, from behind they kind of look like each other," Chico commented. "Look at how their poufy hair bobs up and down in unison. It's even the same grayish-blond color."

"Champagne."

"What?"

"Their hair is champagne-colored."

"Is my hair champagne-colored?" He shot her a winning smile as he flipped his hand through his thick hair like a movie star.

"No, Dodo-head. Your hair is more dirty-dishwater-blond."

"Hmmm. That makes me feel good about myself."

"It's the truth. That's the color of your hair: dirty-dishwater-blond. Just a step up from golden brown."

"Wanda said my blond hair made me look like Robert Redford."

"Oh, you know you are good looking. You don't need Wanda to tell you."

He noticed Talula sounded a bit miffed when he mentioned Wanda's name, so he didn't push the issue. After a little while he took her hand again and she let him. With his other hand, he touched his back underneath his shirt and made certain the gun was still there.

"We need to hide that gun." Talula's comment took him by surprise. Heck, she took him by surprise. She always knew what he was thinking.

"We might need to use it," he said.

"But you can't take it into the store. People might see it and you'll get in trouble," She said with a hint of anger in her voice. "What if the old lady and the poodle had seen it when they passed us back there?" Talula huffed before letting go of his hand. He watched as she wiped the sweat off that had formed on her palm on her jean shorts.

He wished Talula didn't do this thing she was doing where she acted like she liked him like a girlfriend would one minute, then just acted like he was a guy friend that was not special to her the next. Sometimes he just didn't know how to treat her. It embarrassed him how often he misread her. He was such an idiot when it came to girls.

Then he remembered something Miss Lancer had told him. Basically, it was this: we are what we think.

Therefore, think a positive thought every time you start to think something negative, especially when it is a thought about yourself. So, he needed to think of something positive to replace the negative thought he'd just had. But he kept thinking about his idiot thought, then he finally forced a good thought out. Talula seemed to look up to him, and if she thought he was smart enough to look up to and hang around, then maybe he was. Then he thought another good thought to himself: he definitely was getting smarter every day. Not only was he rapidly catching up with the class, he was also learning extra new stuff every day. No one was better than him—that was a fact. No one was better than anyone, really. What was it Miss Lancer liked to say? Each individual has both good and bad traits.

"Just look at Bullwinkle," he thought to himself. That dog probably never had a negative thought about himself not being good enough. He was just happy to be alive and to be in the moment.

Looking up, he saw his grandfather's house. He'd thought it was farther away, but he was relying on the memory of a kindergartner, if he'd even been that old the last time he was here.

"This would be a good place to hide the gun." Chico tilted his head toward the old two-story house. It was large and impressive, even though it had seen much better days. Its wooden exterior was peeling in places and one window had silver foil in it to keep the sun out. He wondered if someone new lived in it now that his grandfather had died. His grandmother had passed on the year before him, and judging from the state of the rose bushes on the side, it probably wasn't a female occupying the old place. In fact, it had an unkempt look about it. It probably was empty.

"We can't just waltz in a house and hide a gun," Talula said. "Where's Bullwinkle?"

"I think he went in the backyard," Chico started toward the side of the house and he felt Talula jerk his arm.

"Do not go in their backyard. That's trespassing."

"Not if you're looking for your dog."

"Okay, we can go to get Bullwinkle, but we can't linger."

Creeping toward the side of the house, they tried to be as quiet as possible. The half-open gate was falling off its hinges. Without moving it, they twisted their slender bodies through the opening. Looking through a window, Chico could see his grandparent's furniture arranged just as they'd left it. And the sight of it socked him in the stomach. He really missed them both.

"It's like a fairyland." Chico felt Talula's whisper in his ear as much as he heard it.

The backyard was filled with shade trees, flowers, and bushes of all kinds. At least three fountains had running water in them. One even had a koi fishpond at its base with lily pad-like things in it. All kinds of colorful flowers bloomed even in the middle of summer, and little concrete pathways ran throughout the garden, dividing it into sections. Upon closer inspection, the pathways had pieces of shell and colored glass mixed in to create a sparkling jewel-like effect. Off to one side was a greenhouse.

Talula put her hand in the spurting water of one of the fountains. Watching her, Chico asked, "Doesn't your name mean 'leaping water' or something like that?"

"Yes," she said.

He stepped back as she waved her hand back and forth, making cool droplets splash in his directions.

"Talula is Native American for 'leaping water.' I used to think my name was Irish or English in origin, but I looked it up in a book of baby names. And that's what it said—a rarely used baby girl's name meaning 'leaping water.' More specifically, it said it was Choctaw in origin."

"Well, it's right pretty," he said as he watched Bullwinkle chasing a large butterfly over to a cluster of colorful flowers. Soon the giant dog had moved into the middle of the low bushes that were chocked full of blooms. It would have made a nice photo if he'd had a camera.

"Look, Bullwinkle's smelling of the lantana," Talula said as she pulled him toward the flowering plants. Suddenly, Bullwinkle stopped sniffing and starting chewing. "No, no!" Talula cried out in a hushed voice as she tried to distract Bullwinkle.

"Good luck trying to boss him around," Chico said as he walked over to the larger of the fountains. It was the one without the lily pond, but it was by far the most beautiful with four large graceful concrete swans positioned just so to catch the water cascading out of its center fountain. Approaching it, he saw the center had a small window in the bottom section. A space where someone could reach in and turn it on and off. He got down on his knees and peered inside. There was a small metal box with a few wrenches in it. Chico mentally measured the box before slipping the gun from his back and putting it inside. "Perfect," he said out loud.

"What are you doing?" Talula's voice made his heart jump.

Pulling back from the opening, he stayed on his knees while staring up at her. He thought about telling her he hid the gun there. He thought about telling her this house used to belong to his father's parents. He thought about telling her, but instead he said, "I'm looking for fairies."

Talula put her hand on his head and gave him a little shove backwards. Smiling, she got down beside him and peered inside. "Look," she said. "It has a switch to turn on the fountain lights. I bet this is beautiful at night."

"It doesn't look like anyone is in the house. Do you want to stay here tonight?" Chico knew they would even as he said it. He and his sister used to love sleeping in hammocks while the fountains danced nearby. His grandmother kept the hammocks in the shed by the greenhouse. Hopefully, they wouldn't be too rotted.

Looking back up at the house, Chico thought it looked totally abandoned. And, for a moment, his heart sank as he thought of the happy times his family had had there.

"Talula," he said. "I have to tell you something. This is my grandparents' old house. My father disappeared around the time my grandfather died and I guess no one in the family took over the place. You'd think they'd have sold it by now. But it doesn't look like it."

As if she sensed his sadness, the always-sensible Talula steered his thoughts back to the present. "Let's go get some food. Then we'll sneak back here as it gets close to dark. It looks like a safe place to hide."

Chico nodded his approval just as his stomach growled.

They only spent ten of Chico's twenty dollars at the little corner grocery store. Talula went over their purchases in her head—bread, peanut butter, crackers and some soda would go a long way. Plus, they got two bear claw pastries for breakfast the next morning.

The sun was just starting to go down as they returned to his grandfather's backyard. She didn't understand why it had taken Chico so long to tell her it was his grandfather's house, she practically had to drag it out of him. But once he told her, he also started to talk about his grandparents, and then he almost started to talk about his father. But "almost" was the key word. He stopped talking and went back into his own thoughts, the way he did when he was ruminating on things. And Talula knew to leave him be.

Earlier, when they had left for the store, they locked Bullwinkle in the backyard and he proceeded to throw one outrageous barking fit. The neighbors probably thought they were torturing him or something. But he was happy to see them now. All ill will was forgotten as he slapped his tail against their legs as they headed toward the greenhouse.

Talula waited for Chico to pull a hammock attached to a metal frame holder out of the corner of the shed. It had been covered with a tarp.

"You know," he said without looking at her. "We should sleep out in the garden under the stars."

"What if Snakeskin . . ."

Chico cut her off. "Bullwinkle would alert us."

Talula reached down and rubbed Bullwinkle's ear. "You're a good watchdog," she said as she scratched around his collar. "You're an angel sent from heaven, you are. But we're going to have to take you back to your owner's house soon. I bet they're worried sick about you."

"This is pretty clean, considering.," Chico said as pulled the big hammock just outside of the greenhouse door. "If we set our bed up here, we can watch the fountain as we go to sleep."

"Think it's strong enough to hold us both?" Talula remarked.

She noticed Chico didn't answer. He went to turn on a faucet on the side of the greenhouse. There wasn't a hose connected and he jumped back when the stream of water got going full force. Bending over where the water didn't hit him, he washed his hands before pouring water in a dish for the dog.

"Oh no," Talula said. "What are we going to feed Bullwinkle?"

"I saw a bag of cat food inside the kitchen just through that window," Chico pointed.

"You can't break in."

"What if it's open?"

"What if someone actually lives here?"

Talula looked at their bag of food. "Dagnabbit it, we forgot a knife. Can't spread the peanut butter without one."

"So I'll go in and get the bag of cat food and a knife."

"Try to find a plastic one."

"Why plastic?"

"Because if you get caught it'll only be a plastic knife not a real one."

Talula saw a weird look cross Chico's face in response to her last statement. But he didn't say anything else as he turned and tested to see if the window would open. It did, and he swung himself up and went inside. While he was trying to get his second leg through, Talula went over to the back door and opened it and went inside.

She couldn't help but stifle a laugh when Chico tumbled through the window at her feet. He was smiling foolishly when he said, "Hey, get your own plastic knife.

I'll get the cat food." A moment later he also added, "And we should probably bring this flashlight." Talula looked over at him pocketing a bright red plastic flashlight.

Then to her surprise, she found a cardboard box of plastic knives in one of the kitchen drawers. Carefully, she only pulled out two. One for Chico. And one for her. That way they wouldn't get each other's germs, she reasoned.

Silently they left the kitchen without ever having turned on a light.

"Is that a piece of bologna in your hand?" Chico sounded incredulous as Bullwinkle sniffed and licked at her hand.

"Yes, I brought it to put on top of the cat food in case Bullwinkle needs enticement."

"I didn't see you open the refrigerator."

"That's because the opened packaged was sitting on top of the counter. This was the only piece left in it." Talula looked over at Chico's shocked face.

"Do you think it's good? Smell of it and see if it's bad. There wasn't anything on the counter when I looked in the window earlier."

"Are you sure?" Talula said with a hint of panic in her voice. "This bologna is still cold. Oh my gosh, someone lives here and they're coming back. They're going to find us."

"Or quite possibly, there's someone in the house right now."

CHAPTER 9

Chico couldn't see his watch, but he could judge that it was somewhere around two o'clock in the morning. Talula was still wheezing even as she slept. He watched the heavy rise and fall of her chest as she struggled with each breath.

Earlier, he had slipped the hammock and its metal holder frame back into the greenhouse, thinking it would keep anyone from seeing them. But now, looking around at the greenhouse they were hiding in, he knew Talula's asthma was only going to get worse with all the pollens, mold, and mildew. Why didn't he think of this before? He needed to move her into the house, and soon, judging by her breathing.

Sitting back, he rubbed his forehead and tried to remember if the bologna had been out on the counter when he looked through the window earlier. There was a possibility he just hadn't noticed it. If that were the case, he and Talula could sleep inside the house without any fear of someone being inside.

Going to the side windows of the greenhouse, he

looked up at the second story of the house. Not one light had turned on all evening. No one had come out to check when Bullwinkle had let out a few playful barks earlier at squirrels. It appeared no one was in the house. But there was only one way to find out—he needed to go through it room by room. Throwing his fears aside, he knew he must help his friend or she would only get worse.

Reaching into his pocket, he took out the flashlight he'd found earlier. He only turned back once to look at Talula's sleeping form curled up on the hammock. Bullwinkle was promptly by his side as he entered through the back door of the house. Carefully, he opened it without so much as a creak. But all the good trying to be quiet did when Chico pushed Bullwinkle back with his knee, the dog let out a whelp. Then as he tried to close the door, Bullwinkle stuck his muzzle in and tried to push past him. "Sorry, Bullwinkle," Chico said as he gently lifted his knee and pushed the dog's nose outside before shutting the door.

Once inside the dark kitchen, Chico gave his eyes a minute to adjust. He saw the glow of a streetlight coming from the front of the house. Treading lightly, he headed into the front living area. It looked the same as it had when he was a boy. Surely, no one was living here.

In the low light, he could make out the old lumpy floral couch and matching loveseat. He remembered his grandfather sitting there reading the newspaper, a metal TV tray nearby overflowing with bowls of various hard candies and a can of mixed nuts. Grampy would always let him and his sister Debra take as many candies and nuts as they wanted. It was their little secret. If it ruined their appetites for dinner, so what? All Grampy cared about was that they were having a good visit.

His throat seized up a little. He wished he weren't so

emotional about the past and about his broken family.

Moving on, he turned and went into the attached formal dining room. His heart thudded a bit as he crept along a nearby hallway, barely bumping a table that held a telephone. If he remembered correctly, there were two downstairs bedrooms and a bath. Upstairs had three bedrooms, a bath, and a library, or something . . . maybe wealthy people called it a smoking room? Goodness grief, he didn't know what to call it. Thanks to his dad's sudden departure, he didn't grow up rich.

What he'd do to live in a house like this? A jolt of jealousy overtook him. How had it been for his dad living his regular life in the likes of this big house? In its day, it had been grand. It still was, to tell the truth, especially the gardens and fountains out back. But, gosh darn, he was living in a trailer. His room was the size of this walk-in linen closet.

Turning the corner, he checked out the downstairs bath.

His heart jumped a little when he caught his own reflection on a mirrored wall in the bathroom. He looked a lot older than he really was, and this thought pleased him. Hadn't Janie remarked earlier on how tall he was getting?

Sneaking back out the hallway, he turned and went up the stairs. The hair stood up on the back of his neck as he took the first few steps. Then he remembered if he walked up on the sides of his feet, his weight would be distributed in such a way that he wouldn't make the stairs creak. It was Talula who had taught him this move in the third grade. In fact, Talula had taught him all sorts of strange things that really worked.

Now he needed to come through for her and take care of her until he could figure out what was going on with Silver, and, of course, the wounded man in the woods. Which by the way, he still didn't believe for a minute was Miss Lancer's brother.

He could only think of one good thing—it appeared they'd thrown Mr. Snakeskin Boots off their trail. But what had happened to Big Mike and Randall? Likely, they'd given up looking for him and Talula. They'd probably returned the white van to church camp by now. Chico only hoped they'd tell Miss Lancer what was happening. She'd know what to do.

It hurt his head to even think about it all. To tell the truth, he was scared out of his mind to be walking through this big old house in the dark trying to figure out if anyone was inside. If they were, they were the quietest person in the world.

The first two bedroom doors were open, so he didn't even go inside, he just sort of peeped in from the hallway. No one was in the smoking/library room either. And, thank goodness, no one was hiding behind the shower curtain in the upstairs bath. Fear left him and confidence started to fill the void as he went further down the upstairs hallway. And, now for the last and final room, which of course had its door closed tight.

Carefully, he considered his options and the most appealing one was to turn back. But he thought of Talula's ragged breathing. She needed to be inside.

Gently, he turned the bedroom door's knob. It didn't budge. He tried again. It was locked. He got down on his knees and looked under the door. Even with the glow of the street lamp shining in through the open drapes, he couldn't see a thing.

Getting up, he decided it would be okay to bring Talula in to the downstairs living room couch. If they got caught, he would make up some story about thinking it was still his grandfather's house if, of course, they didn't shoot them first. He thought of the gun he'd hidden in the fountain and decided to leave it. He'd never be able to explain having Mr. Snakeskin's gun. Plus, deep down inside, he hoped he'd never have to shoot anyone.

Silently, he went back down the stairs and out through the hallway to the kitchen. This time he made it a point to look at the counter to make certain there was nothing on it. Maybe he'd imagined it was empty yesterday. Passing a clock in the living room, he glanced up and saw the clock said 2:13 a.m. just as he'd guessed earlier. He was good at guessing time. He'd have to remember to write this down in his pink notebook since Miss Lancer had asked him to write down every time he had a positive thought about himself. Miss Lancer was a little strange, but he liked the way she was helping him improve in school and in everyday life. As he walked toward the greenhouse to get Talula, he remembered the pink notebook was back at church camp. He'd left it under his mattress when Snakeskin was rushing him along.

Chico debated once again on whether he should wake Talula from her fitful sleep and bring her into the house. Looking back up at the window of the one room he couldn't get into, a little chill ran down his spine. He knew the old house was empty, but he felt it wouldn't be long before someone returned. The air conditioner was turned on low and the house still had electricity and water. If it were truly abandoned, the backyard fountains wouldn't be running around the clock. However, he felt he had to take a chance and bring her inside.

Talula was not fully awake when Chico lifted her into his

arms. Was she dreaming, or was she really a princess being rescued by a knight? Her breathing was wheezy and each breath was a struggle, but being in his strong arms made her feel like everything was going to be okay.

He carried her out the door of the greenhouse toward the back door of the house. Now fully awake, Talula's heart jumped as she said, "Chico! What if the bologna eater is inside?"

"There is no bologna eater. I checked the house out. It's completely empty."

Bullwinkle brushed along Chico's legs, but this time he didn't attempt to go inside the house when the door opened.

"I need a drink," Talula said as Chico carried her inside the kitchen. Her arms were wrapped around his neck and he held her even tighter as he kicked the door shut behind them.

"Alrighty, Missus. I'll get you a drink right after I put you on the sofa," he said as he carried her down the hallway. She was thankful the streetlight showered the hallway with its dim green glow. On the wall she saw photos of a family. It took a moment for it to register that one of the photos was of Chico and his sister when they were little kids. His sister was smiling, revealing the fact that she'd lost her front teeth, and Chico only had on a diaper and a t-shirt.

"Here you go." Chico placed her on the floral couch before covering her with an afghan someone had knitted years ago. Possibly his grandmother, Talula thought. It was gold, brown, and orange and smelled of a faint perfume. It didn't seem musty or anything. Maybe someone lived here on and off, like a vacation house.

After Chico covered her up, he adjusted the couch pillow behind her head.

"How's that?" he said without really expecting an answer.

Then, without another word, he turned to head back to the kitchen. She heard the clink of glasses and the sound of running water. Looking around the room, she felt at home instantly. Chico's grandparents on his father's side must have been nice people.

She remembered Chico telling her he thought his grandfather tried to give his mother money, but she wouldn't take it. All his mother would tell Chico about rejecting his Grampy's generosity was she wanted nothing to do with anyone associated with his father. Talula knew this bothered Chico a lot since he was technically half his father and looked a whole lot like him, or at least that's what Talula could surmise from the one photo she had seen of his father tucked away inside Chico's sock drawer.

The glass of water he brought her had little cartoon characters on it. There was no ice, but really it was better for the water to be room temperature. Her breathing was still uneven. However, she knew it would get better soon now that she was out of the moldy greenhouse. It was too hot and humid in there, and its overload of pollens had been killing her. Being inside with the windows closed and the air conditioner running was the best way to get her asthma under control before it turned into a full blown attack.

Talula observed Chico as he curled up on the matching loveseat near the long sofa she was stretched out on.

"Here," Talula said between sips of water, "I should sleep where you are, I'm shorter."

"No, I want you to stretch out and really sleep." As he said it, he pulled the coffee table closer and put his feet up on it. "I'm going to sleep kind of sitting up, like this."

"Sleeping is sleeping. You're not much of a lookout if you're asleep, so you might as well get comfortable," Talula reasoned.

"I'm not doing it to be a lookout. I'm doing it to think. Sometimes my best ideas come to me as I drift off."

Talula drank more water and contemplated his last statement. "What are you going to think about?" Talula was pretty certain she knew the answer, but she asked the question anyway.

"I'm trying to figure out who to trust."

"Yeah, can't we trust our parents? I vote we call them right now."

"I'm not so sure we should do that."

"You can trust me, Chico." A man's deep voice reverberated through the quiet hallway. Talula was so surprised, she made a shrieking sound. Visibly shaken, she looked up in time to see a dark figure moving down the stairs and out into the living room. The glow from the streetlight lit the man's face as he moved into the room. Her hand shook so, she spilled water on the afghan. But she didn't have to ask who this stranger was; she knew by looking at his mop of dirty-dishwater-blond hair he was Chico's father.

Glancing back at Chico, she saw both anger and recognition flash in his eyes as he looked at the man. As a result, she spilled even more water. "*Oh, shoot,*" she said. Even though she knew Chico thought cussing wasn't attractive, she definitely felt like this was one time he would understand her need to use an expletive.

"How you doing, Talula? I have an inhaler if you need it." The shadowy figure came out into the green glow of the streetlight and handed Talula an inhaler. Still in shock, Chico watched as she examined the label before using it. He saw immediate relief in her face. Yet his anger still overtook him and he blurted out, "What the hell are you doing here?" with a slight tremble that betrayed his emotional state.

"I might ask you the same question," his father said in a calm voice.

Chico didn't know how to respond. The sight of his father after so many years was shocking, yet on some base level he had wanted to find him here, expected to find him here. Then, just as Chico was composing what he wanted to say, another shadowy figure stealthily came down the hallway leading from the kitchen.

"Put your hands up, Sonny," a voice in the darkness said.

The shocked expression on his father's face let him know the stranger was bad news.

Without turning around, Chico watched as his father raised his hands in the air and said, "Arnold, let the kids go. They don't know anything."

"They knew enough to lead me to you, Sonny Boy. I know you've been helping Ben." Arnold, a.k.a. Mr. Snakeskin Boots, said before he shoved his gun into Sonny's back.

Without even thinking, Chico jumped up and did a martial arts move Miss Lancer had taught him. Kicking the gun from Snakeskin's hand, it slid across the hardwood floors toward Talula. Much to Chico's relief, she grabbed it and ran through the kitchen's back door. With another kick and a leg behind Snakeskin's knee, Chico had him on the ground. He sent one more kick to Snakeskin's kidneys and he ran outside after Talula. He found her hiding in the bushes beside the back steps looking down at Bullwinkle's prone body.

"I think Snakeskin killed Bullwinkle," she barely whispered.

"Let's go."

"No, I need to feel for a pulse."

He tried to drag her away, but she persisted in staying by Bullwinkle's side.

"He's alive," she said, looking up to Chico with Snakeskin's gun still in her hand.

"Give me that." He pointed at her hand. "I need to hide it before someone gets hurt."

As he tried to take it from her hand, she pulled back and a metallic swishing sound filled the air.

"Oh my gosh," Talula said. "It's a BB gun."

Relief flooded Chico as he pulled Talula along with him toward the garden gate. He could hear sounds of fighting inside as they ran along the side of the house. Once out in the front yard, he looked wildly up and down the street.

"Hey, it's Snakeskin's car," he said as he steered Talula toward it.

"Shouldn't we be running away from it?" Talula gasped.

"We shouldn't be running at all with your asthma," he said as he slowed to a walk. "Maybe he left the keys in the ignition." As they walked toward it, the hum of the engine became obvious.

"He left it running?" Disbelief and relief filled Talula's voice at the same time.

"Apparently he wasn't going to be long. Wait . . . there's someone in it. Just keep walking. Act like you didn't see the man in the car. Now turn and run into the backyard of this house."

"Which house?" Talula said.

The man got out of the car and started walking toward them.

"Stay here and stall him," Chico said as he ran back to his grandfather's backyard. Quickly, he went to the fountain and started working to get the real gun out from where he'd hidden it earlier. He'd only been gone a moment when he heard Talula shrieking in fear.

Heading back to the front of the house, he saw the man shoving her into his car. Then he watched in horror as the car lurched forward.

Chico ran out into the middle of the street. The driver slammed on the brakes to avoid hitting him. Chico could see Talula's frightened eyes peering at him over the backseat, but he didn't waver; he stood his ground in the middle of the road with the gun pointed straight at the driver's head as he yelled, "Get out of the car, Talula!"

She opened the door and jumped from the backseat.

"Go back to the greenhouse," Chico said in an authoritative yet kind tone. "I'll meet you there in a minute. And Talula, walk, don't run."

"Don't . . . worry. I can . . . hardly . . . walk," she gasped with a mixture of awe and fear in her voice as she headed off.

After he gave her a good head start, he turned to follow her, but the man started to get out of the car to follow him. Chico turned and pointed the gun at him. The man jumped back in the car and left.

"Where'd you get that gun?" A deep voice said from behind him.

Chico was so surprised, he jumped about ten feet in the air before he realized it was his dad.

"Where'd you get that gun?" he said again, only this time in an extremely upset tone.

"It's a BB gun."

"I know," Sonny said. "But the one you've got stuck in the back of your pants isn't."

"The gun belongs to the man you were fighting with. He tried to kidnap us and we got it away from him. Dad, I don't think it's a real gun either. Because when he kidnapped us, Big Mike took it away from him and shot it into a tree accidentally—it didn't sound like a real gun when it fired, it sounded more like a pellet gun. But I'm not sure."

His dad took the gun from Chico's hand and carefully examined it. "You're right, son. It is a pellet gun, but it sure looks real. It's definitely not the gun they used to shoot Ben."

"How do you know about Ben?" Chico cried out in shock.

"I'll explain later," Sonny said as he took him by the arm. "Let's get Talula and get out of here."

"Where are we going to go?"

Just then he looked up to see a drowsy Bullwinkle weaving toward them. Talula followed close behind.

"I think he'll be fine," she called out. "It appears Mr. Snakeskin just gave him a sedative."

"Talula, we have to leave with my dad. We can't take Bullwinkle with us."

"We can't leave him here." She stamped her foot to emphasize she wasn't about to leave him behind.

"Dad, can we take Bullwinkle back to the house where he came from? It's not far from here."

Looking from one to the other, Chico's father assessed the situation. "Sure, just let me get my VW Bug out of the garage. We need to move fast because Arnold might come to his senses at any time. I didn't hit him very hard when I knocked him out."

"We'll wait by the street," Talula said as she guided

Bullwinkle by the collar.

"Be ready to jump in fast when I get to the end of the drive," Sonny said as he ran toward the garage.

Just then, Chico remembered one of the things he liked about his dad: he'd do anything he and his sister wanted, no matter how ridiculous. A pang went through his heart with the memory because he also remembered how sad he'd felt when he finally realized he wasn't coming back. He'd always hoped he would, long past the time he should have. And the anger returned again, making his heart harden just a little more.

In no time flat, Sonny had the VW down the drive.

"Weren't you surprised to find us in your father's home?" Chico tried to sound formal and detached from his dad as he got inside the front passenger seat.

"No, I knew you'd try to come here." His dad's voice cracked with emotion as he took off down the street and turned left. "Your mom called me and told me you two were missing. Seems Big Mike and Randall reported the whole story to Miss Lancer at the church camp and she called your mother and told her everything. She also spoke with Talula's mom, who sent the inhaler prescription to the pharmacy near this house so I'd have it if you two showed up here."

"Mom knows how to get in touch with you?" Chico's voice betrayed him this time. His rage could be contained no longer. "Stop the car. I want out." Even as he said it his father was pulling up to a red light at a busy street. Chico opened the door to get out, but he felt his father pulling at his arm to stay.

"Talula needs to get to a doctor," his dad bargained.

"Take her to one." Chico shook off his dad's grip and bounded from the car, leaving Bullwinkle and Talula perplexed in the back seat. With a quick glance back, he saw Talula bringing her inhaler up to her mouth. His father was right; she did need a doctor. But he needed to get away.

With worry in his heart, he walked away from the car. He knew his dad would get Talula and Bullwinkle to where they needed to be. He was a decent enough guy. In fact, Chico had memories of him being a very kind person. So why had he left them? And why had his mother never let on that she knew where he was? How many times had he seen the pain in her dark eyes at the mention of his father's name? It hurt him just to look at her. Over time, he'd learned not to make any reference to his father at all.

Once, he had seen his mom sitting in her room holding a photo and crying. Later when she was at work, he searched her chest of drawers until he found the snapshot. It was of her and his father when they first met. His father's golden good looks and her dark beauty made them appear to be as different as night and day. Did they really think they'd make it as a couple? He wondered if it bothered his mother that he and his sister looked more like him instead of her. You'd have thought her dark hair and eyes would have been dominant—that's what he'd learned in science class recently. His mother must be a hybrid. Pulling himself together, he tried to stop his tirade of science-related thoughts and concentrate on where he was going.

And then another thought popped into his head: Miss Lancer would have been proud of his dominant and recessive gene observation. Perhaps he would ask her opinion about it when he saw her next. That is, if he ever saw her again.

CHAPTER 10

He was starting to wonder if he wasn't the one messing
things up for himself on this day. He shouldn't have
gotten out of the car. And he shouldn't have left Talula.
He could still see her big eyes looking at him from the
backseat as he dashed down the sidewalk and off into the
nearby woods. It was obvious she was afraid, and he'd left
her. His dad had waited for a few minutes with his
flashers on before he slowly drove off. Chico knew he
would drop Bullwinkle and take Talula to get medical
help, but one side of him wanted his dad to come after
him, to run into the woods looking for him.

"Stupid. Stupid. Stupid," he thought to himself.

Now he needed to figure out his next step. In the
morning, he would call Brother Lowe or Miss Lancer and
ask for their help. It was too late now. Besides, there
wasn't a phone anywhere near, at least not in this little
park he found himself in when he came out of the

117

wooded area. Looking around, he noticed it wasn't much of a park—a few swings and a slide, a couple of picnic tables, and a trash barrel.

Someone had recently held a little kid's birthday party on one of the picnic tables. They'd left the plastic tablecloth on it, held down by big rocks on all four corners. Walking over to it, he sat down. The blue plastic cloth had the words "Happy Birthday" printed all over it with Dalmatian pups and red fire engines. For a moment he contemplated sleeping on the table, then he thought better of it as a clap of thunder sounded in the distance.

The air was already charged in that special way it does before a big storm. He could almost smell the coming rain. Might as well find a good place to make a shelter.

Scooping up the plastic cloth, he let the four big rocks fall to the center. He theorized he should take them with him as they might come in handy. If he didn't need them to hold down the cloth, then he'd use them as weapons to scare off small animals.

Venturing a little way into the wooded area but not so far as to lose his way in the darkness, he stopped under an old tree and sat down on its big exposed root. There he rested his back against the trunk. Looking up, he saw the full moon with a few wispy clouds blowing across it. A puff of air rankled his plastic cloth just before a big raindrop plopped down on his head. He barely had enough time to tuck the plastic over and around him before a barrage of raindrops started to pelt him. They fell hard and fast. In the distance, thunder crashed and lightning cracked. It was definitely going to be a night to remember if he lived through it.

Running away had been a dumb move on his part. He couldn't even think of a good thought to replace this bad one. There was no doubt about it, he'd made a less-than-smart decision, and he had left his pink notebook with all his positive thoughts in it under the mattress back at church camp. It would come in handy now to pump his confidence back up. But, good luck ever getting that back.

Maybe he should go call the hospital and see if his dad and Talula were there. But, on second thought, he'd better stick it out under the plastic. It would be hard to get a ride with anyone in this weather, much less find a phone booth. And he reasoned that he might get hit by lightning out in the open park. No, he'd stay here under the plastic, under the tree, and think.

Squishing his eyes shut, he pondered the multiple questions that nagged at him, like how did his dad know Talula's name? Maybe his mother had told him. Then there was the question of why his mother never told him she knew how to contact his dad. And, the biggest question of all, why would anyone shoot someone over a horse? This wasn't the Wild West.

Settling back against the tree, Chico repositioned the plastic around him. The rain slowed to a drizzle. Sleep was never going to come. His head hurt. His heart hurt. He wished Talula were with him.

Closing his eyes, he imagined her in the hospital. Was she afraid? He knew she tried to put up an image of being brave, but she was often very frightened by unfamiliar situations. If he were with her, he would hold her and comfort her. But he wasn't, and it was his own fault.

Talula waited as Chico's father, Mr. Campbell, or Sonny as he told her to call him, led Bullwinkle up to the gate of his owner's backyard. Bullwinkle must have sensed Sonny was all business because he headed straight inside without any horseplay whatsoever. Watching him return to the car, Talula noticed the way he walked was similar to Chico's gait. In fact, their similar overall appearance made Talula feel less anxious about being left with a stranger in the middle of a thunderstorm. Her breathing was becoming more controlled.

Sonny had left the car running and when he returned, he simply got in and took off.

"How you holding up back there?" Sonny said without taking his eyes off the road.

"I'm better."

"Talula, I need a doctor to take a look at you. I'm going to take you to Brother Lowe's house."

Talula kept quiet. Obviously, Brother Lowe had some kind of medical training if he had helped the man who'd been shot, and going to him seemed like a less frightening choice than going to an emergency room. Plus, he'd probably take her to her parents' house.

Settling down in the back seat, Talula prepared for the ride back. Watching the darkness out of the car window, she thought of Chico as they traveled down the highway. It was surreal—the ongoing blur of white headlights and, in the opposite direction, the line of retreating red taillights; the driving rain hitting the windshield; the rapidly swishing sound of the wiper blades trying to keep up.

"Oh, no. It's starting to rain even harder." Sonny turned on the wiper knob to the high mode as he said it. "I hope Chico finds a good place to take cover."

At least he was worried about the son he had abandoned. Talula thought about what it must be like for Chico out in this storm. Mr. Campbell was right; the rain was intensifying. Lightning crashed and thunder rolled. Maybe someone had picked Chico up and taken him somewhere safe, or maybe he found some kind of shelter. The thought of him shivering out in the open in this driving rainstorm was incomprehensible.

"Maybe we should go back and look for Chico," Talula found herself speaking her thoughts out loud.

"How are you doing?" Sonny's voice wavered.

"I'm okay."

Sonny whipped a U-turn, and they headed back to the area where Chico had gotten out of the car. It took a while to get there, and she noticed Sonny kept running his hand through his thick hair when he wasn't clenching the steering wheel.

"Talula, how much do you guys know?" Sonny looked up into the rearview mirror so he could see her face.

She didn't answer.

"I can't help you if you don't tell me."

121

Silence.

Talula, why were those two guys after you kids?"

Considering her options carefully, she finally decided she needed to tell an adult about what had happened at Silver's shed.

"We were feeding Mr. Jamison's horse, Silver, out in the country when we heard gunshots at a nearby trailer."

She hesitated.

"And . . ." Sonny said in a patient tone.

"And the two guys at your house are the ones who fired the shots. They saw my bike and Chico's pogo stick when they came out of the trailer," she hesitated before continuing. "And one of the men remembered we had been outside the trailer earlier. But, thanks to Chico's quick thinking, we hid in the feed shed so they couldn't find us that day."

She decided this was enough information, but Sonny decided it wasn't. "But Chico went back to the trailer later that night."

"How did you know that?"

"His mother told me."

Now Talula knew for a fact that Chico did not relay this information to his mom. So it only meant one thing: Sonny was in on the situation with Snakeskin and his pal. She remembered thinking it was odd Snakeskin had known Sonny's first name, and Sonny had known Snakeskin's first name was Arnold. But, she reasoned, it could be because Sonny and Arnold grew up in the same area. The two probably went to the same school.

Gathering her courage, she continued. "Chico went

back, but he didn't find a thing." Talula left out the fact he had found a person. After all, a person wasn't a thing. No need to give Sonny all the facts at this point in time until she was sure she could trust him. Besides, Sonny was pulling the car up to the intersection where they had let Chico off and he seemed to not be paying attention to her story anymore. In fact, he was looking wildly around for any sign of his boy. But the rain was pouring in sheets, making a dark curtain all around them.

She saw Sonny reach under his seat for a plastic packet. Unzipping it, he pulled out a folded raincoat. Shaking it open, he put it over his head instead of wearing it. "Wait here," he said before popping his door open and jumping out into the storm.

Talula heard him yelling at the top of his lungs, "Chico, I'm sorry! I'm sorry, son!" But she knew her friend probably couldn't hear him over the thunder and lightning. Still he called. And called.

Carefully, she looked around at the nearby park and woods. If she squinted her eyes and looked really hard, she could make out picnic tables and a line of trees, but no sign of Chico. Even the street light near their car was muted to a dull gray in the downpour. She'd never seen weather like this before with its deafening roar of crackling thunder bolts.

It seemed to be the storm of the century. Still, Sonny continued to yell, "Chico! Chico! I'm sorry, Chico!" The name carried on the wind, but Talula doubted anyone other than herself heard it.

Little rivers of water ran under Chico's body. He watched as two of the rivulets beside him grew significantly larger, which really didn't matter because he was already wet through and through. In the distance, it sounded like someone was calling his name between peals of thunder. For a moment he thought it might be his dad. But then his heart hurt a little when he realized his dad would never come back for him. If Sonny really wanted him, he'd have never have left in the first place.

Before his dad abandoned their family, Chico had trusted him completely to take care of him and his sister. That's what made his leaving so hard to take. If he had been a bad dad, so to speak, maybe Chico could have dealt with his leaving better. But as it was, his leaving only served to make him feel less secure and more stupid at times like this. And he'd been doing so well at thinking positively and changing himself for the better.

Well, no one was going to come to the rescue tonight, so Chico decided to get up and start walking toward civilization now that the storm was subsiding. Wrapping the plastic tablecloth around his drenched, shivering body, he stood and walked toward the area where his dad had let him get out of the car earlier that evening. Mud sucked at his shoes. Water ran down his face. Good, it would hide his tears. Thunder rolled as he strained to hear if someone really was calling his name.

Just as he came out of the tree-line, he saw his dad getting back in his car. Running frantically, Chico tried to yelled for him to stop. For a moment he thought Talula saw him as she peered from the back of the car in his direction, but apparently she didn't, because the car started up and drove slowly away, abandoning him once again.

"Damn," he cried.

Cursing didn't do much to make him feel better. So he stopped.

And he looked around.

It was time to take charge of the situation.

For some reason he kept asking himself why anyone would shoot Ben, the man he found wounded in the woods? The thought occurred to him he should go back to his grandfather's house and confront Snakeskin outright about the matter. Or at least he should go back and sneak around until he found out why Snakeskin and his pal would shoot a man over a horse. Silver didn't seem to be any kind of special horse and, to be honest, he didn't even live in a barn. He had a simple little carport and shed, a shed that was the storage area for someone's trailer.

With his head down, Chico walked the same streets he had walked with his grandfather when he was a small boy. "Chico Boy," he could almost hear his grandfather call out to him as he swung him up in the air and let him ride on his strong shoulders. Other times they just held hands as they meandered along to the park. "Chico Boy. Oh, my dear Chico Boy," his grandfather would sing. Yes, being a little kid with a grandfather like his had been a great experience. So, what had gone wrong? Why did his father leave them? Why did his mother keep them from seeing their grandfather?

Then as they always did, his thoughts turned to Talula. He hoped she was okay.

Talula was surprised Sonny had changed his mind about taking her to Brother Lowe's house. Instead, he had taken her to the nearest emergency room and called her camp counselor, Miss Lancer.

Miss Lancer arrived in record time with the health papers her mother had signed giving her the right to get treatment. She watched from a gurney as Miss Lancer gave the nurse her parent's insurance information. The nurse had a tense expression on her face as she surveyed the documents. As Talula listened in on the exchange between Miss Lancer and the nurse, another doctor came up and introduced himself.

"May I check your breathing?" he said as he held up his stethoscope. Without even waiting for her answer, he placed the cold metal on her chest underneath her gown. Moving from the front to her back, his face grew concerned as he asked her to breathe deeply once more.

"Let's get her into treatment ASAP." The doctor's voice was calm but stern as he spoke to two orderlies.

Then in two seconds flat, she was being rushed down the hallway. Sonny got up from his seat on a hard metal bench and followed them until they reached a pair of steel doors.

"You'll need to stay on this side," the doctor explained as he opened up the chart he was holding and started to make notes. Turning to Talula, he said, "Are you allergic to anything?" It took a moment for Talula to realize the doctor was talking to her. She was too busy watching Sonny being left on the other side of the doors. He looked so concerned and so much like Chico, her heart ached. What was happening to Chico outside in this weather? Was it possible he found safe shelter?

"Tell him," Talula's wispy breath hardly came out, so the doctor leaned in closer. "Tell him to go get Chico."

"What?" She knew by the doctor's expression he was confused.

"Tell him. Take care of Chico."

One of the orderlies said, "She wants us to tell him to take care of someone."

"Can you make out the name?" the doctor asked.

"I think so. Is it Chico?" The orderly looked at Talula as the doctor was putting an oxygen mask over her pale face.

She shook her head yes.

The orderly squeezed her hand gently and said, "I'll be right back." Then he took off through the big steel doors. Talula watched as they slowly closed behind him. Then she turned her attention to the doctor. He was drawing up a shot and preparing to give it to her.

"Wow," she tried to say, but only a small wheeze came out. The shot hurt, but she didn't cry. From experience, she knew it'd only make her breathing worse.

Little did she know that outside the steel doors, the orderly was still trying to find Sonny. It seemed he had virtually disappeared. Finally, he went to the emergency room entrance and asked a couple just coming in if they'd seen him outside.

"Yes," one of the people said. "We saw a tall blond man get in a VW Bug and take off."

The other person gestured toward the road. "He headed to the highway that runs through town. And he was driving pretty fast in this horrible storm."

The orderly cast one last futile glance at the almost empty parking lot and went back inside. He decided not to tell her he wasn't able to deliver the message. It would upset her and that's the last thing someone in her condition needed.

CHAPTER 11

Creeping around the side of his grandfather's house, Chico found a window to spy through. The warm, humid rain had made it foggy, and when he reached up to wipe it clean, he discovered the fog was on the inside. But he could still see through enough to tell the window latch was not locked in place. "Perfect," he thought. Luck was on his side. As the next clap of thunder roared, he slid the window up, and before the thunder subsided, he had already stepped inside and closed it behind him.

His wet shoes creaked as he moved down the hardwoods in the hallway, and his clothes left telltale droplets of water as he moved into one of the interior rooms. He stopped and listened. Every muscle in his body poised to strike out.

He was not alone.

A gruff man's voice approached the dark room where he was hiding. However, the person did not enter, they only lingered at the door momentarily before moving down the hall. Still on high alert, Chico heard a closet door open and shut. Before too long, he heard the owner of the gruff voice moving back past the study door. Chico peeped out after he'd passed just long enough to see the man was carrying something in his hand—a phonebook—and he was wearing snakeskin cowboy boots. Oh, no . . . it was Snakeskin, and he had someone with him.

Straining to hear, Chico realized the two people were ordering pizza. He listened as they discussed what they wanted. They argued over anchovies before Snakeskin said, "Go ahead and order it the way you want it. I'll pick the anchovies off." Then the other man's voice politely said that he could do without anchovies. "Funny," Chico thought to himself, "these two didn't seem so tough. In fact, they seemed like okay everyday guys." But Chico was positive they had been the same two men at the horse shed the day he and Talula heard Ben get shot. Those snakeskin boots were unlike any others.

Why did they shoot Ben? Why? It didn't make sense. Judging from what Chico had seen in Ben's trailer that night, he was just a gizmo-scientist-type guy that liked to work on his projects. He seemed harmless enough.

Listening intently, Chico heard one of the men say, "Arnold, let's listen to the weather report. It's getting bad out there." The radio crackled and hissed to life. Chico heard the words "severe storms" and "high winds." Moving closer to the study door, he strained for more information.

"Maybe we shouldn't order pizza," the gruff voice sounded like Snakeskin Boots. "Wouldn't want anyone to have to deliver it in this rain."

"I could make us some bologna sandwiches," the other man said.

"We had that the other day when we were watching those kids. Is there any left?"

"Nah, I think I left the rest of it out on the counter when we had to rush out of here. It wouldn't be any good now."

Chico heard them opening and shutting cabinets in the kitchen.

"Here's some canned stew," Snakeskin said. "I could put it over some mashed potatoes, make shepherd's pie."

"That sounds good. You want me to make the mashed potatoes?"

Then, to Chico's surprise, they started to sing as they cooked. It sounded awful. But it made the perfect opportunity for him to retrieve some dry clothes from his grandfather's closet.

Plodding along the wooden hallway in his bare feet—turned sideways so as not to make any loud creaks—he went up the stairs and turned left into a bedroom. Opening the closet door, he got a whiff of the spicy aftershave his grandfather had worn daily. It made Chico sad for a moment as he realized all of Grampy's clothes were probably just as he had left them, all lined up and waiting for him to come back.

Carefully, he selected a pair of dark-colored pants. He was surprised they weren't that big on him. Wow.

Talk about a growth spurt. He was almost as tall as Grampy, and that meant he was also almost as tall as his dad. He wondered if his dad had been surprised at how tall he'd gotten in the year since he'd left. Pushing back dark thoughts just as Miss Lancer had taught him, he turned his attention to a big chest of drawers. Inside he found a plain white t-shirt. Quickly, he took off his soaked shirt and pulled the dry one over his head. Looking in the mirror, he arranged his wet hair with his hands, and that's when he saw him—or rather, he saw a person's shadow moving along the hall wall.

Slowly, without a noise, Chico crouched down and waited for the big man to pass. Moving down on his knees, he hid behind his grandfather's bed and listened. His heart pounded so hard, he thought his chest would explode. Taking a deep breath, he slipped under the bed. A clock ticked by the bedside table. The timbers in the old house moaned and creaked under the strain of the powerful winds. And downstairs, he heard one of the two men start to sing again.

What was he singing? Chico strained harder to hear the lyrics. *Everybody was Kung Fu Fighting?* He couldn't believe his ears. The guy singing was pretty good when he didn't have Snakeskin joining in and throwing him off key.

"Hey, is that shepherd's pie close to being ready?" Chico recognized Snakeskin's voice over the other man's vocals.

"Yeah, let's give it a couple of more minutes to heat in the oven."

That was the last of the polite conversation. Suddenly, he heard dishes breaking, furniture being tossed around, and every now and then he heard someone grunt, groan or yell out in pain. The noise level got so bad, he knew he must do something. Especially when he heard one of the men say, "Sonny, you think you can take the two of us? We have guns."

Chico thought of Ben's wounded shoulder. These men could've easily killed him if the bullet had landed a little more to the right. He knew without a doubt they wouldn't hesitate to shoot his father. And Talula? Where was Talula? Was she hiding upstairs or was she safe in a hospital?

Without a moment's hesitation, Chico left his fear behind. Bounding down the stairs, he ran through the hallway to the kitchen. Sliding around the corner, he saw Sonny holding his hands in the air while both men held a gun on him. Relief flooded his father's eyes when he recognized him.

Before Snakeskin and his pal could even react, Chico flew into action, popping the guns out of both their hands with a couple of well-placed karate kicks. Then Sonny sprang into action, but he didn't use martial arts; he went for good old-fashioned punches. Before long he'd clocked their blocks, knocking the lights out of Snakeskin's friend before wrestling Snakeskin himself to the ground.

He couldn't have been prouder of his dad. True, he didn't start the fight, but boy, he sure did finish it.

Scurrying around, Chico gathered up the two guns.

Just as he suspected, they weren't real. In fact, they were very similar to the BB and pellet guns he'd taken from them a few days ago. They looked real, but they were fakes.

Putting the guns on the counter, he got duct tape out of one of the kitchen drawers and walked over to his father who was still holding Snakeskin down in a headlock. "Where's Talula?" Chico asked as he ripped a strip off to bind the man's hands.

"She's at the hospital," a female voice said from the den. It was Miss Lancer.

How in the world did Miss Lancer get in his grandfather's house? Was he hallucinating? Or dreaming? If so, this dream was weirder than his nightmare about climbing a meat mountain on a motorcycle. It certainly had just as many hurdles to overcome in it.

"Miss Lancer! What are you doing here?" He choked out in surprise.

"Talula told me to come here. She's in the hospital with an asthma attack," Miss Lancer said as she moved into the warm light of the kitchen. "I've called her parents to come and take her home. The doctor should be releasing her soon."

The aroma of almost-done shepherd's pie filled the air. Chico watched as Miss Lancer went over and checked the oven's timer. Grabbing a mitt, she expertly opened the oven door and took the flower-embossed Corning Ware dish out. Sitting it on a trivet on the counter, she left it to cool. Nearby Snakeskin still struggled underneath Sonny's headlock as Chico loosely taped up his feet, giving him just enough room to walk, but not run.

"Chico, you could also use duct tape to secure Mr. Simpson to this chair," Miss Lancer said as she pointed to a straight back wooden chair at the kitchen table. "Just in case he gets any ideas of running away."

"We're out of duct tape," he said, holding up an empty cardboard cylinder. "But I know where there's more. It's in Snakeskin's—I mean, Mr. Simpson's—car. He used it to tie up Talula when he kidnapped her." As he started down the hallway toward the front door, he heard his father say in exasperation, "Arnold, you tried to kidnap Talula? Why on earth would you do a thing like that? Why, I ought to have finished you off back in high school when I had the chance." Snakeskin said something back, but Chico didn't have time to stay and listen.

He opened the door and went out into the dark night. Down the street, he could make out the outline of a parked car and he was pretty sure it belonged to Mr. Simpson. Chico shook his head. Since when did he start thinking of Snakeskin as Mr. Simpson?

The storm had turned into little more than a drizzle, even though occasional lightning still flashed overhead. The night air held a chill and it was giving off a positive vibe as it was super-charged with negative ions from the rain. He'd learned this from a science magazine article. He must remember to tell Talula this fact; she would be impressed.

Chico observed Miss Lancer as she securely wrapped

Snakeskin's hands with duct tape to the chair. Turning to address Chico, she said, "Now, let's tape up his passed-out friend. But first, please help me stretch this man out on the couch so he'll be comfortable when he wakes up."

"He'll be fine," Sonny said. "I hardly touched him."

"He is rousing already." She put her fingers up to the man's neck and checked his pulse. "Let's just leave him here and secure his hands and feet." After she finished securing the other man, she looked up and said, "Chico, would you put this tape away for me?"

He took the tape and put it back in the drawer. His dad stood nearby with his hands on his hips and an angry look in his eyes, staring down at Arnold Simpson.

"Would you mind feeding me a few bites of shepherd's pie?" Arnold asked his dad.

Sonny looked down at him in wonder. "You want me to feed you after you shot at my kid?"

"I never shot at your kid. It was my partner, Sam, over there," Arnold said, gesturing with his head toward the man on the floor. "Sam is the one who carried a real gun that day. He's the one that got us into this mess. If he hadn't had a real gun when we went to the trailer to scare Ben, then he wouldn't have accidentally shot him in the shoulder."

Chico watched Sonny move to the kitchen cabinets and get out four bowls. As his father put them on the table, he listened carefully to what Snakeskin was telling them.

Arnold continued. "When I begged Sam to go back and check on Ben later that night to make sure he was okay, we encountered your son coming out of the trailer. Sam shot in your son's direction to scare him away. He thought Chico might be helping Ben, maybe even hiding him since he was nowhere in sight."

Chico couldn't take his eyes off Sonny as he got four spoons and a ladle out of the drawer. It was obvious he was used to the layout of the kitchen. Chico wondered how many family meals he'd helped prepare here in the past. He watched as his father served up the steaming bowls of shepherd's pie each with a spoon in it.

Across the room, Arnold was still explaining his side of the story. "Later, I attempted to nab Chico and Talula at church camp," he said, "because I was trying to find out where Ben was and if he was still alive. I didn't want to be responsible for someone's death. I didn't want a murder rap. And I wouldn't have hurt the kids. Didn't even have a real gun. It was a pellet gun, but it looked real enough. So I know it scared them . . . and I'm sorry for that, but I was going to let the kids go as soon as they told me what I wanted to know. I swear, it's the truth."

Arnold stopped talking and hung his head before continuing. "So does anyone know if Ben is okay? Have you heard from him?"

"Yes," Sonny said as he moved forward and spooned a few bites from the bowl into Arnold's mouth. "Ben survived and he's still working on the project."

"Thank God," Arnold said sincerely.

Suddenly, Sam stirred on the floor. He'd come to his full senses.

In an anger-filled voice, he spat out, "Don't you guys

know how many people Ben will put out of work if he succeeds with his Super Stamina Feed formula project? Not just the thousands that work for V-Labs, but people all over the world. Vets and medical facilities for animals. Do the math . . . it's simple. If animals aren't getting sick very often, they aren't going to need very many of the medicines we manufacture. In fact, they may not need them at all."

"But Sam," Arnold interrupted, "we can't think that way anymore. We almost killed a man instead of just harassing him to stop his project, all so we could save our jobs. Don't you see? It wasn't right what we did. And now we're probably going to see jail time."

Chico could not believe what he was hearing.

"This just freaks me out!" he yelled out to no one particular in the room. "Of all the confounded reasons to shoot a man. Here I've been worrying Ben must have been doing something sinister for you to shoot him. And Miss Lancer and my father were in on it. But no, you two are after him because he's trying to help animals—help the world."

The room was silent as Chico sat and fumed.

Finally, he spoke again, this time in a more civilized tone. "Mr. Simpson, you did scare Talula and myself really bad, but I think we can both forgive you in time. No one was hurt. So maybe things won't go so bad for you."

"But you, sir," Chico said as he pointed a finger at Sam, "you will probably have to go to jail for a long time. You did shoot Ben, even if it was an accident. And those rounds you shot at me got pretty close, even though you said you were shooting at the ground." He stooped down and moved closer to Sam's face. "Did you ever stop to consider that Ben's Super Stamina Feed formula might create new jobs at the same time it was making others obsolete? Maybe not as many will lose jobs as you think." Chico waved his hands and his voice became louder. "Did you ever even think at all?" He glanced over at Miss Lancer as she poured herself and Arnold a glass of water.

Still on his soapbox, he continued ranting. "And you two," he said pointing at Sonny and Miss Lancer. "How do you two know so much about this? Miss Lancer, I thought you were just a really nice substitute teacher. And Dad, I thought you were gone for good. "He saw Miss Lancer look down at the floor. His father on the other hand, chose to look directly at him.

"Chico," he started, then stopped. "There's a lot I can't tell you, but I can tell you this: I didn't abandon you; I was sent on a job overseas—dangerous mission. And Miss Lancer here—Jillian—well, she was on the same team as me with about twenty other people. We had just completed our work when Jillian came back here to marry her fiancé." He wasn't used to hearing anyone using Miss Lancer's first name and it took him by surprise.

Still looking at the floor, Miss Lancer spoke to him. "Chico, Ben is not my brother, he's my fiancé. Your father was the one that introduced me to Ben. Just like Arnold and your dad, they go back a long way." Looking up, she continued. "I lied the night Ben was shot because I wanted to protect his identity. And I wanted to protect you. I didn't want you to know too much."

"Ha," Chico snorted. "I knew Ben wasn't your brother. His southern accent and your midwestern one. You two couldn't look more different."

Miss Lancer spoke again, only this time she looked him directly in the eye.

"I took the substitute teaching job here in hopes of making it a permanent one. So Ben and I could be together after we got married. Only thing is, as soon as I got back, Ben told me some of the employees at V-Labs had been harassing him, trying to stop his work on the new feed." She shot a quick look at Sonny, before turning back to Chico. "I knew if anyone could help keep Ben safe it'd be your dad, and," she hesitated, "I knew how much he missed your mother, how much he wanted to be back with his family. So, I called him to come help Ben. Good thing I did because the day after he got here, Ben went missing. That's when I found you two in the alley."

"Go on," Chico said. "Some of this is starting to make sense. Except for the part about my dad wanting to come home." He waved his empty spoon in Sonny's direction. "If my father was so worried about us, how come he left in the first place, without so much as a goodbye? Just slipped away in the night. No letters. No phone calls. No way on contacting him because he didn't tell anyone where he was going."

Just as Sonny was about to open his mouth to speak, someone pounded on the front door. The only person in the room that didn't jump out of their skin was Miss Lancer; she just calmly got up and padded down the hall to the door.

"Wait," Sonny said. "You don't know who it is. They might be more V-Lab folks."

Even though he was afraid, Chico got up and followed her to the door.

"It's Ben," she said as she looked through the peephole. "I called him just before I left Talula at the hospital. Wanted him to know I was coming here to see if Chico might have returned to this house after he ran away." Opening the door, she motioned Ben inside. "Promised Talula I'd find Chico. Finding you Sonny, and these two criminals, was just extra."

Chico saw Ben step inside. And then to his surprise, Brother Lowe stepped in right behind Ben and closed the door.

A few seconds later, another knock came at the door. His heart jumped again.

"Oh, yeah," Miss Lancer said, "I also phoned Ben and told him to call the police when you went out to Arnold's car to get the duct tape, Chico." Standing aside, he let her guide the three policemen down the hall before following them. Once inside the kitchen, the head officer turned and asked him which one of the men had shot at him. He pointed at the man duct-taped on the floor. "He did, Officer."

"He was trespassing," Sam said angrily.

Chico's heart leapt. But Ben came to his rescue. "No, I'm the tenant of the trailer, and I say he wasn't. However, you two were trespassing," Ben said forcefully as he pointed at Sam and Arnold. "And this one here shot me in the shoulder at point blank range."

The next few moments were a flurry of activity as the officers cut the duct tape off of their two suspects and replaced the restraints with handcuffs before reading them their rights. As they took Sam and Arnold down the hallway toward the patrol car, Arnold looked back at him and said, "I'm sorry." Behind Arnold's head, Chico saw a flurry of red and blue lights flashing through the sheer draperies in his grandfather's living room. It made a pit form in Chico's stomach. He knew the man was truly sorry, but it wasn't going to help him get out of the deep trouble he was facing.

Coming back to the kitchen area, Chico watched Sonny sit back down at the table. "Eat your food, Chico," he said, "while it's still warm." Following his father's example, he sat down and began to eat. If there was one thing he admired about his father, it was that he never let pressure get to him.

"It's good, huh?" His father nudged him as they ate side by side.

"Hey, son," His father continued between mouthfuls, "that was some show you put on back there when you kicked their guns away. I have to tell you, I was impressed."

"Miss Lancer taught me that move," Chico said as he flushed with pride.

"I tell you, Sonny," Miss Lancer said as she put her bowl down and wiped her mouth with a paper towel, "your kid is good. He's as fast as you."

CHAPTER 12

She checked the clock on the wall again. Chico had said he was coming over to get his stuff at two o'clock in the afternoon. "Good," she thought. She still had another hour to rest.

Earlier that day, she and her mother had gone back to the church camp to get their belongings. Randall had helped them gather Chico's things from the boys' dorms. He'd even reminded her to look under the mattress for Chico's pink notebook.

"How'd you know that was under there?" Talula had asked him.

"Well," he stammered, "as you can see, my bunk is right above his. I saw him putting it under there." Randall gave her an I'm-so-guilty look. "Don't worry. I didn't read it."

Changing the subject, Randall asked, "What about your suitcase? You were carrying it when you got kidnapped, weren't you? I think I saw you running down the alley with it."

"Yes," Talula hesitated. "I had it with me in the back seat of the car. I grabbed it when I escaped. And I threw it in some bushes near Bullwinkle's fenced backyard. Mom's going to drive me over to try and find it." She shook her head. "Hope I can remember which fence. All I know is it was near the Dairy Royal."

"I think I can find it," Randall offered. "Remember, I'm the one that drove the white van when Chico and Big Mike were looking for you. I think I can take you right to it."

On the car ride back to Bullwinkle's yard, Talula's mother drove and Randall pointed out where she needed to go. He was so polite, using his nicest voice to say things to her mother like, "You need to slow down now, Mrs. Moonstone, because your turn is coming up in about a quarter of a mile." There wasn't even a trace of the overbearing bully he was a few weeks back. Talula thought to herself, "Chico was right—Randall's changing for the better." Maybe all he needed were a few good friends like herself, Chico and Big Mike.

Talula stared out the window at the passing scenery. It was pretty with its fields of wildflowers and flowing grasses, but it was also very flat and she could see Indian Paintbrushes and other native Texas wildflowers for miles and miles. Before too long, a small town popped up on the horizon, and all too soon they were pulling into the

Dairy Royal parking lot where she'd escaped the kidnapping. Being there gave her a creepy feeling.

"Here," Randall pointed. "Go down this alley in the back. It leads into a neighborhood. And if I remember correctly, it was only about eight fences down where I let Chico out of the van."

Her mother drove very slowly as Talula and Randall looked at the fences.

"Was this the clump of bushes?" Randall asked.

"I don't know," Talula said from the backseat. "All these bushes and wooden fences look very similar. Let me get out and check."

Talula waited patiently as Mrs. Moonstone steered the car to the side of the alley and put it in park. But Talula noticed she didn't dare turn the air conditioner off as the temperature was nearing 100 degrees. Hopping out, she immediately felt the force of the heat pushing down. As she walked over to the clump of bushes, she saw the edge of her colorful suitcase peeking out, and not too far down the fence line, she heard a dog snorting and sniffing. Pulling her suitcase to her, she walked a little farther down the alley.

A joyful 'woof' called out to her from the other side of the fence.

"Bullwinkle?" She cried out.

"Woof. Woof." The big dog answered back as his tags jangled.

Looking down, she saw Bullwinkle's big square nose jutting out of a hole in the fence where a wooden slat had broken off, probably from years of him pressing his nose against it. Getting down on her knees, she spoke softly. "How have you been, buddy?" Rubbing his velvet nose she said, "Good ole Bullwinkle. I wish I'd thought to bring a treat for you."

Through the loose slats of the weather-beaten fence, she could see Bullwinkle's behind wiggling as he beat his long tail against the grass. "Sweet boy, if only your parents knew what an adventure you had with us. Maybe one day I'll write a story about you. Would you like that? I bet you would."

"Talula?" It was Randall. He'd come up behind her while she was talking. "Talula, your mother wanted me to remind you that she needed to get me back to camp so you two could get back home before Chico comes over at two o'clock."

As they walked back to the car, Randall took the suitcase from her hand and said, "I think you should write a Bullwinkle story. I loved the animal story you told on the bus the other day."

"You were listening to my story?"

"Yes," he said. "I was sitting on the other side of the aisle. Remember?"

"That's right, you were."

Opening the back door, he tossed her suitcase inside. "You can ride up front with your mom since I rode shotgun on the way here," he said as he opened the front passenger door for her. "Go ahead. Get in," he said in a most gentlemanly voice. Was this really Randall, the school bully, talking?

The cool air vents blasted Talula's face as she jumped

in the front seat.

"Man, does that feel good," she said as she lifted her long hair up off of her neck. "It's hot as Hades out there."

"I have an idea," her mother said. "Why don't I pull through the Dairy Royal's drive-thru for ice cream?"

"Yes," Talula and Randall said at the same time.

Chico thumbed the pages of his pink notebook as Talula put his suitcase on the oversized ottoman in her den.

"I think Randall and I got everything," she said. "You can thank him for remembering your notebook."

He watched as she unzipped the suitcase's top pocket and pulled out his old stinky sneakers, complete with duct-taped soles. "Wheeew-wee!" She waved the tennis shoes near his nose. "I'm going to take these to the outside trash bin."

Putting down the notebook, he grabbed his nasty sneakers from her. "Here let me do it," he said as he made a run for the back door, holding the sneakers in one hand and his nose with the other. "They're so foul, I don't want you to gag yourself to death. I can just hear it on the nightly news: 'Talula Moonstone falls over dead from noxious sneaker stench.'"

Outside near the alley, he smelled the aroma of decaying trash as he tossed his rank shoes inside the big silver metal can before slamming its cover back down. A horsefly buzzed nearby and he heard birds singing in the big live oak overhead. For a moment, he stopped and gazed down at the shoes Big Mike's mother had given him. Thankful. Grateful. Appreciative. Words couldn't express how glad he was to have them on his feet. One day soon he would offer to do something nice for Big Mike's mom. Maybe weed her garden or something.

"Chico," Talula called from the back door. "Come here, I want to show you something."

Running back up to the porch steps, he felt these almost-new shoes really did make a difference in his sprint.

"What is it?" he said.

"The autograph book you took to camp," she said as she held it out for him to see. "Look inside. There's writing."

Taking the small leather bound book from her, Chico went back inside to the den and sat on the couch. "Here, sit beside me," he said as he patted the couch cushion beside him. Talula hesitated.

"Sit here," he patted the seat beside him again. "Let's read it together." This time Talula sat down—about a foot and a half away from him. He gave her a look and she moved closer. He gave her another look and she moved even closer until their shoulder's barely touched. Taking turns, they unfolded the pages in the small faux-leather book and read the mysterious autographs out loud.

"*Matthew, Mark, Luke & John were here.*" Chico laughed out loud as he read the first entry.

"*Great swimming with you! Noah,*" Talula giggled over the inscription on the second page.

"*Peace Out! Zechariah*" This one brought a laugh and a snort from Talula.

Chico had to wait for her to recover before he read the next page.

"*Stay cool. Timothy 1.*"

And turning the page, he read, "*Stay cooler. Timothy 2.*"

"Here give me the book," Talula said, pulling it from his hands. "*Peace & Love. Your best friend, Esther,*" she read out loud. "And look, it has a little mod flower drawn on it."

On and on it went with autographs from Ruth, Thaddeus, Hosea, Isaiah and Ezekiel. Until they got to the end. And the last page read. "*Hey, Chico Boy! Thanks for being my friend. Randall.*"

The smell of chocolate chip cookies baking wafted into the den. Talula heard her mother rattling around in the kitchen and knew it would only be a matter of minutes before she was ready to serve them. Apparently, she saw Chico as a special guest and had gone all out getting ready for his visit. But Talula didn't mind if that meant fresh baked cookies.

"Hey," she said. "Let's go see if those cookies are ready." Chico got up and followed her through the swinging doors to the kitchen. Her mother had the cookie pan on top of the oven and she was using a spatula to lift the piping hot cookies off one at a time onto a plate. She looked up as she worked and said, "You two sound like you're having a lot of fun in there."

"We are," Chico said as he sniffed the air and rubbed his stomach. "Randall wrote some funny things in my church camp autograph book and we were reading it."

"See, Talula? That's why you should've brought an autograph book. I told you we should've packed everything the counselors put on the list."

"Okay, Mother, if you say so."

Changing the subject, Talula went to the refrigerator.

"Chico, you want water, soda, or milk with your cookies?"

"Milk," he answered. "There's nothing like chocolate chip cookies and milk."

"I agree," said Talula's mother. "And now if you'll excuse me, I'm going to take a few of these cookies into the den and watch my soap opera."

Talula and Chico watched as her mother pushed her way through the swinging kitchen doors, balancing a plate of a cookies and a glass of milk. It was obvious to them she did not want any interruptions during her favorite show.

Turning to Chico, Talula said, "I guess this means we'll be eating in here. Unless you want to watch the latest of episode of *The Young & The Lonely* with my mom."

"Here is fine," he said as he pulled up a chair and sat his icy cold glass of milk down on the table. In no time flat, he'd woofed down two of the cookies.

Sitting at the kitchen table, Talula listened to everything Chico told her about Snakeskin and his pal, Sam. Man, talk about crazy. It was unthinkable Ben had been shot for trying to improve animal feed. Never in a million years would Talula have guessed that was their motive. Even though both men claimed it was an accidental shooting, she was happy to hear they were both locked away awaiting trial. True, she didn't think Arnold, a.k.a. Snakeskin, deserved as much jail time as Sam, but she did think they both were guilty. She and Chico could have gotten hurt when they were on the run. If not for Sonny's quick action taking her to the hospital, she'd be in a lot of trouble right now. As it was, the doctors were able to control her asthma with medications and they let her mother take her home. Sonny had quite literally saved her.

Which brought her to another question she'd been wanting to ask him.

"Chico," Talula approached the subject with caution. "What about your father?"

"What about my father?" he said.

"How did you feel about finding him at your grandfather's house?" She stopped and started again. "You know, how are things between you two?"

"I guess things are about as okay as they can be between a father and the son he mysteriously abandoned."

Trying a different tactic, she said, "What did he say to your mother when he took you home?"

"He didn't say much, but she did. You should have heard her accusing him of putting me in danger. I've never heard her yell like that before."

Talula saw him withdraw into himself and knew it

151

was time to stop questioning him. Instead she said, "Want to help me make some more of these chocolate chip cookies?"

"You know how to make cookies from scratch?" he said with wonder.

Going to the refrigerator and taking out a tube of cookie dough, she said, "Not exactly. I prefer to cook my cookies the way my mother and her mother do—I slice pre-mixed dough in a tube into sections and lay them out on a cookie sheet to bake for thirteen minutes. But here's our little family secret that makes them so good: we really take them out at eleven minutes because it makes them gooier."

Talula watched him as he picked up the tube of cookie dough.

"Not that I don't trust you," he said, "it's just Miss Lancer says you need to read directions all the way through before starting a project so you won't mess it up at the end because you did something the wrong way up front."

"You know, Chichi," Talula said affectionately as she wrapped an apron around her, "you really are making progress in the intelligence department. I always knew you had it in you."

He hung his head and put the dough back down on the table.

"Guess my dad leaving so abruptly got me off track and threw me behind at school. Then once I was behind, I got more behind every day until it was almost impossible to catch up . . . you know what I mean."

She nodded before getting a big knife out of the sink and washing it off. It was the same one her mother had used to slice the cookies so it wasn't very dirty. It just needed a little rinse before she dried it with a cup towel.

"Talula," he said in a quiet voice, "parents splitting up is worse than you'd think. It's kind of like someone died. That's how it makes you feel. Because your family died really. You don't have it anymore. Even though all the family members are still alive. It's different. I don't even know how to say it better than that. I just have this awful feeling inside when I talk or think about it." She wasn't sure she knew exactly what he was trying to tell her because she'd never experienced what he was going through. So she went over to the table near him and said, "I hear you, Chico Boy. I hear you." When he reached up to put his arm around her, she hugged him back.

Walking back home with his suitcase in hand, Chico thought about how strange it had been to see his dad the other night and how normal it seemed all at the same time. Sonny was still the same man, still talked the same, acted the same; it was hard for Chico not to let him back into their lives.

What did his dad mean when he said he was sent to do a mission overseas? He thought his dad worked for V-Labs like everyone else in town. although he did have to admit he thought it was strange the few times he'd seen his father strap on a gun underneath his sports coat. And what about the time the union was picketing V-Labs and

Sonny kept crossing their line every morning and going to work? When Chico had asked him why, he just answered, "I'm not part of their union."

In fact, the more Chico thought about it, the stranger his dad's job seemed to him. He never talked about his work, at least not in any detail. One time Chico remembered his dad coming home from work looking bushed. His mother was finishing cooking, and he and his sister were sitting at the table waiting for him to get there so they could start eating. But when he came in through the door, he wasn't his normal self. He looked beaten down, like he was carrying a heavy weight on his shoulders.

"How did it go today, honey?" he remembered his mother asking.

And his dad had said, "No one got killed today, so I guess it was a good day." At the time Chico thought he was just being funny. But now, he wasn't so sure.

Whispered conversations between his parents in the night when they thought he and his sister were asleep now were starting to make sense, especially one of the last ones he'd eavesdropped on right before his father left. His mother had said, "As long as you're making a living with a gun in your hand, don't come home. It's just too dangerous for the kids and me. If you go on this overseas mission—you'd better stay gone."

As Chico walked, he realized he'd been thinking so hard, he hadn't even been aware of his surroundings. He'd come to his trailer's front door almost on auto-pilot. Inside he could hear his mother and sister laughing. This was a good thing as his mother didn't laugh much anymore.

CHAPTER 13

The clock near his bed read ten o'clock p.m. when the phone rang and woke him up. Although not terribly late, he'd fallen sound asleep listening to music on his headphones in bed. He still had on his jeans and t-shirt.

Chico slid on his stomach over the low shag carpet in their trailer's hallway. If he kept low, he could position himself near the entrance of the hall so his mother wouldn't see him from the kitchen. Staying as quiet as possible, he strained his ears to eavesdrop on her phone conversation. It wasn't easy to hear her soft voice. Unlike his sister's voice, it didn't carry.

The loud sound of the phone's shrill ringing had jerked him out of his dreamlike state and he'd almost fallen out of bed onto the floor before he recovered. *Thanks, Debra.* He thought to himself how a few weeks back, his sister had set the ringer to its loudest volume option so she wouldn't miss a call from one of her many friends. It was so loud, the people in the trailer next door had complained to his mother that they could hear it. But Debra had insisted on keeping it that loud so she could hear it even if she was in the shower.

"What if Chico or you needed me," she pleaded with their mother, "and I couldn't hear the phone?" In fact, she was so insistent on being able to hear the phone from the shower, his mother had given in and left it at its ear-splitting level.

But tonight it wasn't Debra's phone call. The call was for his mother and she was talking in a serious tone. And that's why he'd deemed it necessary to listen in on what she was saying to the mysterious caller. Moving around, he found a more comfortable position in the hallway with his back up against the wall and his arms around his knees that were pushed up to his chest.

"I don't think so," his mother said forcefully into the phone receiver.

He heard the deep voice of a man talking on the other end.

Reaching down, he pulled on the new orange shag carpeting, making it twist this way and that between his fingers. The carpet was the only thing new about the trailer. Well, that and the water heater their landlord had to replace when it had broken down and flooded the hallway last fall. The landlord was a thoughtful man and he'd let Chico's mother pick out the color carpet she wanted when he replaced it. Everyone had been a little surprised she'd picked bright orange as she was usually very practical and picked decorating hues that would merge with any color scheme. But he noticed she'd been getting bolder in her life choices lately. And, so was he. He hoped he was making his mom proud by getting back on track in school.

Finally, his mother started to speak again. He had to strain to hear her.

"Sonny, you can talk all day. I don't want to hear it."

The voice on the other end said something.

Then his mother said, "Goodbye! Goodbye! I'm hanging up now, Sonny."

Peering around the corner, Chico watched as his mother put her face in her hands and began to cry. Without a second thought, he got up out of his hiding place and went to her side.

"Mom," he said as he put his arms around her. From out of nowhere, his sister appeared and did the same.

Brrrrriiiiiinnnnnnng! The phone blasted off the wall. Chico grabbed it, thinking he'd hear his dad's voice on the other end. But he was wrong; it was their next-door neighbor. They'd called to tell them their phone ringer was still too loud.

"Yes," Chico stammered. "I'm lowering the volume right now."

His mother started to laugh. He was thankful to see her smile.

"I can't believe old nosey Nelda can hear our phone," Debra said. "She probably never even gets a call. You'd think she'd enjoy listening to ours ring once in a while."

"Now, Debra," his mother said only half-joking. "It's

not every once in a while. You live on that phone. That's why we got the extra long cord, remember?"

"I thought we got the long cord so she could do housework while she talked," Chico said.

He thought back to how Debra had begged their mother for the extra long phone cord. However, instead of using it to do cleaning, she ended up using it to stretch out on the couch in the den, usually with a bowl of potato chips and a soda while she chatted with her many friends.

How many times had she left the dishes for their mother to do after she came home from work? Whenever Chico tried to bug her about it, their mother waved it off and said, "Leave her be, Chico. She only gets to be young once. She'll be doing more than enough housework in her adult life."

The situation had made Chico so mad, he'd started doing a lot of the housework, and his mother had noticed. She always thanked him and told him what a nice job he was doing. He'd hoped his sister would get the message and start to help, but she never did.

"So, who was that you were talking to on the phone earlier?" Debra said nonchalantly, trying to change the subject.

"It was your father." His mother's smile faded to a grim line and her eyes lost their glow.

"Is he coming home?" Debra asked with hope in her voice.

"No, he's not." Their mom shut her down flat.

One glare from her dark eyes and they both knew better than to ask their mother anything more about their father's phone call.

Talula was careful to measure out the right amount of feed for Silver. She was surprised Mr. Jamison had needed her pet sitting service again so soon. She'd taken care of Silver the week before church camp when he'd gone to visit his sister in Alabama, and now he was off to a trip in the Panhandle for his cousin's wedding. Seems the old man never went anywhere, and then all of the sudden, he was globetrotting all over the place.

"Silver seems a tad sad, doesn't he?" she said to Chico as she poured the fresh feed in the horse's trough.

"He's just missing old Jamison."

Talula patted the horse. Then, turning the horse's face toward her, she talked directly to Silver. "That's all it is, ole boy, isn't it? Because we know you aren't sick, thanks to the fact that your diet for the last year has been Ben's new Super Stamina Feed."

"Hey, how does it feel to be a guinea pig?" Chico also spoke directly to Silver.

"He's not a guinea pig!" Talula was indignant. "He was the first ever trial participant for Super Stamina Feed."

Ignoring Talula's last statement, Chico once again spoke to Silver, "How does it feel being the first ever guinea pig horse?"

Shaking her head at Chico's latest nonsense, she said, "I imagine it feels alright. Seeing as it keeps him immune to most common illnesses."

"Just think, Silver," he continued talking to the horse, "you're one of the first animal's ever to experience Ben's innovative feed formula. You're historically significant."

"Listen to you," Talula exclaimed. "I swear, every time I turn around these days, you're spitting out fifty cent college words."

Spontaneously, she stood on tiptoe and put her arm around his shoulder. Squeezing him in a half hug, she said, "I'm real proud of you, Chichi."

The term of endearment wasn't lost on him.

"Yeah, I feel real different about myself these days. And I can see you feel different about me, too. Before today, you'd never have gotten within an inch of me, much less hugged me." Pulling back from her embrace, he gazed directly into her eyes. "What I want to know is—were you afraid of me? Or afraid of having a boyfriend in general?"

Talula stood awkwardly by the trough, saying nothing.

"I'm not going to let you off the hook. I want an answer," he said as he gently turned her face up towards his.

Time seemed to stand still as they stood by the water trough gazing intently into each others eyes in the ninety degree heat. Then, just when it seemed like they might kiss, Talula turned away.

"I think I was afraid of your stinky tennis shoes," she said, breaking the magic spell. But he wasn't to be deterred.

"Ahh, I know you like me," he said as he went to turn on the nearby water spigot before picking up the attached hose and giving her a little spray. "In fact, you're so hot for me I think I need to cool you down," he said, turning the water pressure higher at the spigot.

"Just fill up the water trough," she said, shielding her face from the spraying hose. "My pet sitting service does not pay employees to make bad jokes while goofing off."

"Okay, okay." He said, turning the spewing hose toward Silver's water trough. "Don't want to make the boss lady mad on my first day of work." Using his thumb at the opening of the hose, he made the clear cold water spurt upwards like a little fountain of sorts. It reminded Talula of the fountains in his grandfather's backyard. It seemed longer than a week since they'd been there.

She wondered how things were progressing with Arnold Simpson and his pal Sam. Their small town grapevine had reported that the men were going to be sent to a federal facility for a couple of years. And she'd also heard word on the street was the V-Labs' President and the upper level executives were busy coming up with alternative ways to make extra profits. Through these new ventures, they could afford to back Ben's Super Stamina Feed research without worrying about losses from their Veterinary Pharmaceuticals division. Which meant no one would be losing their job anytime soon because V-Lab executives speculated people all over the world would be eager to buy the new feed for their animals. Perhaps they wouldn't make as much money off of the feed as the medicines, she reasoned, but they would still make a fortune, and it was a win-win for people and animals.

Looking out over the distant tree line, she strained her eyes to follow the trail of a small rabbit as it ran for cover from a predator hawk. Secretly she prayed that the bunny would make it, and he did. Turning to Chico, she said, "Hey, thanks for being there for me last week . . . protecting me," she reached out and touched his arm. "I may not have looked like it, but I was scared silly. And uh . . ."

"What?"

"Nothing."

"What?" his voice sounded concerned.

"Your muscles are getting big." She laughed out loud as she touched his upper arm again.

Grabbing a Pop-Tart for breakfast, Chico put his pink notebook in his bag and prepared to go to the church for algebra tutoring. Now that Miss Lancer had helped him catch up with his grade, he was really getting into math. In fact, he was very good at it and he wanted to take honors math when real school started again. But this morning, he had to move fast if he wanted to get to tutoring on time. The bus didn't run in the summertime, so he'd have to hoof it on foot.

Earlier he had asked his father if he could have the old bike in the garage at his grandfather's house. His father had told him sure, but it wouldn't fit in his VW Bug when it came time to bring Chico home, and there was no way to tie it on the outside without scratching the paint.

But this morning apparently his father had found a way to get it to him. As he opened the door, he saw Brother Lowe's pickup in front of their trailer. Sonny was around back, getting the bike out of the truck bed. His father took off an old blanket he had wrapped around it for protection, then he put the bike on its kickstand in their driveway. A big smile lit Chico's face. Finally, he had a set of wheels. Not the cool ten speed he'd been looking at in the store, but an older three speed bike, a little rusty with peeling paint in places, but a bike nonetheless. Now he could ride free all around town. It was better than his long-lost pogo stick, by far. Even though he did still miss the pogo stick. Curses to Arnold and Sam for taking it.

Just as he approached the bike and threw his book bag over the handle bars, the trailer door behind him squeaked opened. Turning, he saw his mother standing at the flimsy trailer door with her bunny pajamas on and her hair in pink sponge rollers. Her hands were on her hips, and her dark eyes threw daggers in his father's direction.

"I told you not to come here, Sonny," she said angrily.

Just when Chico was sure the situation couldn't get any worse, Debra's face peeped over his mother's shoulder. "Daddy," she cried, giving a little wave before his mother pushed her back inside and closed the door.

"Debra," his father called out as the door was shut. "I love you, honey."

Inside the trailer, Debra called back, "I love you too, Daddy." Thank God for non-soundproof trailers. Chico thought to himself that his father deserved to know his children loved him, even if his wife didn't.

Turning toward Brother Lowe, he said, "Here, would you like to have my untouched Pop-Tart? It's still warm."

Brother Lowe looked at the Pop-Tart for a full thirty seconds before he said, "Yes, I would. If you're not going to eat it, that is. Wouldn't want it to go to waste."

Chico handed over the Pop-Tart and then got off the bike. Taking his book bag, he walked back up the rickety steel steps leading to the trailer. Opening the door, he poked his head inside and said, "Mom, I think you need to ask Dad to come in so he can visit a few minutes with Debra." Then he turned to his dad and waved him up the steps.

Brother Lowe said, "Hey, Sonny. I'm going to run. Call me and I'll come back to pick you up when you're ready." With that, he got in his truck and backed down the gravel drive, being careful not to hit the bike standing on its kickstand in a nearby patch of dirt and grass.

Sonny passed Chico on the rickety metal step. Opening the door, he went inside.

Chico waited for a minute. When he didn't hear any yelling, he went down to get on his bike. But then he had second thoughts as the voices inside got louder, so he moved back toward the trailer. Standing frozen on the first step, he could hear Debra as she talked with their father whom she hadn't seen in over a year. Her voice was high and animated. Clearly, she was overjoyed. His mother's voice was lower and more muffled. He could hardly make out what she was saying. It sounded like she was offering Sonny a Pop-Tart. And, not so surprisingly, his father was accepting it. In his mind's eye, he envisioned all three of them sitting at the little Formica table in the kitchen eating breakfast. Just like old times, only it wasn't. He'd better go inside if he ever wanted to see that happy family scene one more time. Judging by his mom's tone, she wasn't going to let this Norman Rockwell moment last long. Boy, he sure wasn't expecting this to happen now.

Taking a deep breath, he tugged the metal door open. All three of them turned and looked at him. Awkwardly, he entered the kitchen and stood there, like a lump on a log or something. He was feeling kind of sick, kind of nervous, and jumpy. He didn't know what he expected to happen, but mentally he was trying to prepare himself.

"Daddy, please come home," Debra said as tears began to form in her eyes. "Please," she pleaded. "I'll obey all your rules and I promise not to sneak around. Chico and I'll be good if you just come back."

"I didn't leave because you kids were a problem. I left because of my work."

No one said a word. In fact, no one moved. The toaster popped up Debra's frozen waffles, but no one made an attempt to get them. It was obvious she was in no state of mind to eat.

"Sonny, you didn't have to go overseas on such a dangerous mission." A storm started to brew in his mother's dark eyes as she spoke. "V-Labs offered you a regular job—a *regular* job like *regular* people have with *regular* family lives."

The tension in the air was so thick Chico felt like he'd explode. He didn't like drama. Especially this kind of drama that might determine his future in the next moment.

"You put us in danger," his mother's voice rose with her anger. "You're addicted to danger. You have to feel the adrenaline. You can't be normal. You can't live a regular life anymore. You're too far gone." As the hateful words spewed from her mouth, Sonny looked like he'd been slapped. He didn't try to retaliate in any way.

And Debra started to cry harder.

"Don't fight, don't fight!" his big sister screamed. "Mother, why can't you let us visit for just a little while. Is that too much to ask?" she cried out before jumping up from the table and running down the hallway to her room. Now Chico's eyes started to brim with tears.

But his mother would not be deterred. She'd held this anger inside for a long time, not just over the past year, but possibly as long as she'd been married. "Your work has always come first," she shook a fist in the air. "Why'd you even marry me? Why'd you have children? How could being a husband and father ever be enough for you?" With that, she picked up a bag of flour off the kitchen counter and threw it all over Sonny.

Okay, this was unexpected behavior, Chico thought as he shielded his mouth from the cloud of white dust settling in the air. *Did this really just happen?*

Reaching out to stop her from doing anything more, Chico said, "Why did you do that?"

"I don't know," his crying mother answered as he hugged and comforted her like a parent would a small child. "I'm the one that will have to clean it up."

His father sat still in his chair. Covered head to toe in white flour, he still held his Pop-Tart in his hand. "This would be funny under different circumstances," Chico thought as he grabbed a cup towel from the drawer and went over to hand it to him. His father looked utterly defeated. Taking the small colorful towel from Chico, he stood and wiped his face clean.

"May I use your phone?" he said calmly. "I need to call Brother Lowe to pick me up."

From the far back bedroom, Chico could hear his sister crying her eyes out. Over the years, he'd realized the more upset she became, the more she made a snorting sound as her sadness overcame her. She was doing that now, and the sound of it made his eyes water a little more. In fact, the whole scene made his throat ache, he guessed from tensing up his throat muscles, or maybe his heart was in his throat and it was a heartache.

Getting a paper napkin, he placed Debra's two waffles from the toaster on it. They were stone cold, but it didn't matter. Debra wouldn't be eating them anyway. Bringing them to her would be an excuse to get away from the scene that was still playing out in the kitchen.

He watched as his mother stood glaring at his father in front of their Harvest Gold refrigerator. She held a wooden spoon in her right hand like a weapon. It appeared the angry storm inside her was spiraling more out of control by the second.

Chico had never seen her so mad. Not even that time when he'd gotten green goo all over Debra's white Easter dress, or when he'd pulled up the antique flowers that had just sprouted because he thought they were weeds. Yes, he'd seen her fume, but he'd never seen her blow her top like this. It scared him all the way down to his core.

For a moment, he considered staying in the kitchen to make certain no one got hurt. But then Sonny turned away and walked right out of the door and out of their lives.

Chico saw the door didn't close all the way behind him, so he went to shut it himself. And when he did, he caught a glimpse of his dad—not just walking away, but sort of running away, as if he ran fast enough he'd escape the grief of experiencing love die. But Chico couldn't run. He had to stay here and pick up the pieces.

Taking a deep breath, he turned back to look at his mother who was heaped over on the kitchen floor. Her shoulders shaking violently in silent sobs, the wooden spoon still clutched in her fist. Quietly, he set Debra's cold waffles on the table and bent down to comfort his mom, not by talking, because there weren't any words that'd make things better. Instead, he sat beside her and gently stroked her back.

CHAPTER 14

"I have to check in on the Stevens' rabbits and feed Mrs. Churney's two collies." Talula reviewed her handwritten pet sitting service to-do list in front of Chico. "But I can do both of those things after we meet Big Mike and Randall for ice cream." Going over to her bike, she said, "We're supposed to meet them downtown at two o'clock." With that, she threw her leg over the banana seat on her bike and put her foot on one pedal. "Let's roll."

Chico hopped on his new-to-him bike and started pedaling. Slowly, he moved the gear shift. A horrible noise came from the old bike as he switched directly from first gear to third.

"Chichi, sounds like you're grinding hamburger with those gears."

"I know," he laughed. "Just haven't learned how to use them yet."

"You'll get the hang of it."

She watched as he moved up through the gears until it was hard for him to pedal because it was so stiff. Slowly, she rode along beside him, just watching. She didn't want to disturb him while he figured the gears out for himself. But it was hard not to say anything as he struggled to ride.

Finally he looked up and saw her watching him.

"Speaking of grinding hamburger," he said slightly out of breath, "riding this bike right now reminds me of the 'Meat Mountain' dream I had. Just like now, it was so hard to move forward."

"Let's figure these gears out before you hurt yourself or someone else," she said, pointing to the gear shifters on his bike.

Talula steered her bicycle off to the side of the road and stopped. Chico followed her lead.

"First, I want to tell you something," he said. "Let's leave our bikes here and sit on these big rocks."

And so it was that Chico spilled to her all that he'd been through that morning with his family—how his father brought the bike over in Brother Lowe's truck, how his sister wanted to visit with their dad so he talked his mom into letting him come inside, and, last but not least, how his mom blasted his dad by dumping a full bag of baking flour on him.

Talula tried to smother a giggle when he described the attack. "I'm sorry," she said. "But you have to admit, it's kind of funny. You know she didn't really want to hurt him or she'd have thrown something much more toxic."

"That's just it," he said. "She still loves him. And he loves her. But they have this obstacle that they can't get past."

"Like your meat mountain dream."

"Except I've gained headway on the obstacles in my life. These two can't even find common ground to stand on. All they do is fight."

Talula moved over on the big rock so that she was close enough to reach up and rub Chico's shoulder. "You know what? I think your parents will work things out and get back together. Your mother is still mad that he went overseas. The whole thing scared her. They'll get back together."

"No, Talula. I really don't think so."

Neither said anything for a while after that.

She left him to his thoughts and stared out to an open field just beyond where they were sitting. Tall grasses waved in the breeze and birds circled overhead. Bright, puffy, white clouds floated on a true blue sky. A Texas sky that stretched out to infinity. It was hard to feel Chico's sadness on this beautiful day as she sat right beside him. She might not be able to help him feel better, but she wouldn't leave him to go it alone.

Finally, he said, "On a different subject, when I was at my grandfather's house, just before the police took Arnold Simpson away handcuffed, he asked me to tell you he was sorry for scaring you. He wanted you to know he's not like that. That he had no plans to harm you."

"Umm," she said, "I'm happy he's sorry, but I

disagree. He *is* like that or he wouldn't have done it."

"I thought that, too, but my dad said something that changed my mind," Chico said, looking over at her. "He told me after the police took Arnold away that he really wasn't like that growing up. He could be irritating at times, but overall he was a decent guy. However, he did have a tendency to act without thinking and to follow the crowd. So it wasn't that surprising that he'd followed Sam into trouble without thinking about the consequences of what would happen if they tried to bully Ben. They didn't plan on doing more than scaring him, but they almost killed him.

"Then Miss Lancer got in on the conversation and she said, 'Trouble often starts out that way. You make one small bad decision and before you know it, its escalated to a lot of bad decisions and you're in too deep to get out.'"

Talula sat silently digesting this explanation.

"You see," he continued, "a person can end up quickly doing things that they thought they would never do."

"How did your dad get so wise?"

"He said he had learned this the hard way, and he was trying to head it off for me. Told me to always carefully consider if something was right or wrong and then try to choose right. Because small mess-ups snowball into big ones before you know it."

They both sat and considered the weight of this last statement for a moment before Chico got up and said, "Enough of this serious stuff. Let's go meet up with Big

Mike and Randall before they think we've stood them up."

In the distance, a dog barked a warning. Talula knew it meant someone was coming up the road. As she picked up her purple Stingray bike, she peered in the direction they'd ridden from. "Look," she said. "I think its Randall."

Before they got back on their bikes, the person was upon them.

It was Randall.

"Nice bike, Chico," he said sincerely.

Talula looked over at the bike Randall was riding. It was about the same age as Chico's and a very similar model. "Perfect," she thought as she said, "Randall, can you help us figure out the gears on Chico's bike?"

"No, Talula, I will not help you figure out the gears on Chico's bike, but I will help Chico," Randall said sarcastically as he pulled alongside them. She thought to herself that Randall wasn't the bully he used to be, but he was still a bit of a jerk. Oh well, at least he was entertaining at times with his odd sense of humor. His autograph prank had rated high on her laugh meter.

While Randall gave Chico a short tutorial on gears, Talula rode on ahead to the Ice Cream Palace. The sun beat down on her head. Up ahead, she saw a mirage spreading across the paved road. She knew it wasn't really water, but the thought of it made her pedal faster to get to their final destination. With a glance behind her, she saw Chico and Randall gaining on her. Slowing her speed, she decided to let them catch up. She didn't want to overdo it. She'd wear herself out, then she might have trouble breathing. She didn't want that to happen because today was her birthday. She wanted to have fun and be without a care in the world on her special day.

So when Chico and Randall sped past her, she didn't even try to keep up. "Life should not be a competition," she thought as she kept riding at her own pace—doing her own thing.

Chico was the first bicycler to arrive at the Ice Cream Palace, followed by Randall. Standing his bike up on its kickstand, he looked around. Big Mike was already there, sitting at one of the outdoor tables. He had something in his hand.

"Hey, Chico," Big Mike said as he stood and approached him. "Got you something."

He held up a thick chain encased in orange plastic. It had a rotating number lock on the end.

"What is it?"

"It's a lock for your bike."

"How did you know I got a bike?"

"Brother Lowe told me. Here, let me show you how to use it." In a graceful swoop, he put his long arm around Chico's front tire and looped it through, then he brought the chain around the nearby lamppost before locking it. "Now get down here. I'll show you how to unlock it."

Chico bent down near him and observed as he rolled the numbers, feeling for a click as he went. "Were you able to memorize the numbers?" Big Mike said.

Chico nodded affirmatively.

"Let's see you give it a try."

After a couple of false starts, he got the lock to open easily.

"And I got Talula's gift for you to give her." Big Mike reached into his pocket and brought out a small box wrapped in neon pink gift paper. "Look, my mom even wrapped it for you. She said stuff like that is important to a girl."

Chico took the package and hid it behind his back. He couldn't believe it when his mother had insisted he keep the leftover money from the emergency twenty she'd given him for camp. After buying food at the little grocery by his grandfather's house last week, he'd had just under ten dollars. Just enough to get Talula a birthday necklace from the Burke's store. He'd given his money to Big Mike to buy it for him so he could surprise her today.

He could see Talula pulling up to the Ice Cream Palace. As she put down her kickstand, she said, "What's up? Why are you guys staring at me weird?"

"Huh . . . um," Chico cleared his throat before walking toward her. When he was a couple of feet away from her, he brought out the brightly wrapped gift from behind his back.

"Happy Birthday!" his voice cracked.

Talula stood stunned. She wasn't expecting a present. A big smile spread across her face as he handed the small package over to her.

"Open it," Randall said impatiently.

Without more prodding, she tore off the pretty bow and began to unwrap it. Big Mike stepped forward and took the bow and paper from her. He then tossed it in a nearby trash can like he was dunking a basketball.

With great anticipation, she opened the velvet jewelry box for all to see. Then, she made a little screaming noise as she brought her hand up to cover her mouth.

"Oh, it's the necklace that I saw in the store window," she cried. Literally, tears sprang to her eyes. Then, throwing her arm around Chico's neck, she hugged him close. "Thank you. Thank you so much."

Randall poked his head near Chico's and Talula's to take a look at the necklace. "So does this mean you two are promised?"

Talula blushed. "I'm too young to be promised," she said as she stepped away from both Randall and Chico.

"Maybe we can just say we're promised to be promised to be engaged one day," Chico said as he took the small jewelry box from her. "Here, let me put it on you."

Awkwardly, he took the small heart necklace from its satin lining and undid the hook. Talula lifted her long hair from her neck and held it up on top of her head while turning her back to Chico. Carefully, he laced it around her neck and hooked it with one try. Still blushing, she turned around for all to see.

"Just what Talula needed in her life," Randall blurted out. "A relationship with a good man." Talula immediately reached up and thumped Randall on the head.

"What?" he cried out. "That's what you told Janie you wanted when you two were sitting together on the church bus to camp. Can't help it if I was sitting close enough to overhear every word."

Chico smiled at her and took her hand. "Let's go eat some ice cream and celebrate."

Big Mike opened the door and ushered their small group inside.

"Hey, Chico and Talula." It was Miss Lancer, and she had Ben by her side. "Randall, Big Mike. How are you guys?" Without waiting for an answer, she motioned to the man beside her and said, "Look at Ben here. He's doing great." It was true, aside from having his arm in a sling, Ben did look in good health. Much better than the night Chico had met him in the woods.

"Just the man I wanted to see," said Ben. "I wanted to thank you for helping me out when you found me wounded in the woods. Your actions were very brave."

Quietly, Chico said with a smile on his face, "I think we both know I wasn't that brave."

"No, I think you were. The fact that you were afraid but went ahead and helped me makes you that much more brave in my book. Let me buy you kids ice cream. I insist." Ben went up to the counter and told the girl at the register, "It's all on me. Whatever they want." Then he turned back to Chico and said, "I can afford it, thanks to my new position at V-Labs. Not only did they hire me back, they're making a whole new division for my Super Stamina Feed, thanks to you. Arnold told them all about how you suggested they save jobs by expanding instead of just producing vet medications. Arnold also confessed as to how he and Sam had harassed me to the point where I had to quit my job. And how they had gone to the trailer where I was hiding out so they could stop my feed trials with Silver."

Miss Lancer popped over with a double dip chocolate cone. "Ben's not the only one with new digs for work. Silver's getting a state-of-the-art horse stall along with ten other horses. V-Labs is going big with Super Stamina Feed. They predict it's going to be huge."

Chico shook his head. "Wow, and to think Sam almost killed you to keep from losing his job."

"He didn't see the big picture," Miss Lancer said as she quickly caught a drip of ice cream with her tongue. "If he had taken Ben's work to his superiors instead of firing him, he might have been promoted himself instead of being put behind bars."

The girl at the register gestured in Chico's direction. "You're next. What'll it be?"

"Just one scoop of plain vanilla in a cup for me," he said.

"Get some sprinkles or something," Big Mike said. "We're celebrating Talula's birthday,"

"And Ben's new promotion," added Miss Lancer. "And Chico, you know the test you took to be placed in Honor's Algebra? You passed it with flying colors."

"Alright." Chico felt his chest swelling with pride. The day may have started out really bad, but it was getting better by the second.

"I'll have chocolate syrup and sprinkles, please." He

said to the girl behind the counter.

With dread in his heart, he opened the trailer door and stepped inside. It appeared no one was home but himself. He listened and all he could hear was the steady hum of the air conditioner. As he moved closer to the window unit, the vents rushed icy cold air over his flushed hot skin.

Riding his bike home from the Ice Cream Palace had been a life-changing experience for him. He had pedaled hard and practically flew down the road. His mood soared with his newfound mobility. But now he was overheated and dehydrated from his effort, and a little sore, to tell the truth.

Headed into the kitchen for a drink, he saw it was spotless. Not a bit of the white flour dust remained to be seen. As he poured himself a glass of tap water, he overheard his mother on the phone in her room. Her voice sounded upbeat, almost joyful. This surprised him as he had left her sitting on the couch with a box of tissues earlier that morning. Guzzling the water, he stopped still in his tracks and listened.

She sounded a lot like his sister. The tone she was using sounded the same as Debra's when she was having one of her serious talks with her boyfriend. Was it Debra on the phone or his mother? Quietly, he moved across the orange shag carpet in the den and went down the hallway toward Debra's room. He could use her phone to listen in on the conversation. As always, Debra's door was closed. A big yellow sticker at eye level read "Proceed with Caution." He knew his sister would kill him if she caught him in her room, especially if he used her extension to listen in on a private phone conversation. But he had to know who his mom was talking to. Without a second's hesitation, he turned the knob, opened the door, and peered inside. Much to his surprise, Debra was stretched out on the floor listening on her extension to their mother's conversation. Great minds think alike, he guessed.

She had the phone receiver turned up away from her mouth so her breathing wouldn't give her away. Fortunately, she was so engrossed in her snooping that she didn't notice him. He watched her for a full minute before entering the room. In a pile of dirty clothes near her bed, he saw the outfit she'd been wearing that morning. It was one of her favorites and it was covered in white flour dust. Did Debra clean up the mess in the kitchen?

The world was getting weirder by the minute. Debra didn't ever clean. She left cleaning to the mere mortals of the world. In other words, she left it to him and his mother. And, he was embarrassed to admit it even to himself, but his mother usually did most of it.

As he approached Debra from behind, she rolled over on the shag carpet and looked up at him, bringing a finger to her lips in the universal "shhh" sign. Carefully, he sat down cross-legged on the floor near her and observed as she listened in. He could hear the voices through the receiver. Obviously, one was male. Did his mother have a boyfriend? He'd never known her to talk to a guy on the phone. But then again, she thought he was out of the house.

His sister reached up and pushed her thick hair back. She had flour on the back of her hand and it got in her hair. He knew better than to mention it. He just sat still like a statue.

Reaching out for a pen, Debra wrote across an open page of a nearby notebook. He looked down at her graceful cursive. It read "Mom is talking to Dad."

Taking the pen from her, he scratched out, "Are they getting back together?"

"They're talking." She wrote back. "He's apologizing. She's accepting."

Holding her finger up in the air in the universal sign for "wait," Debra listened intently, and her face lit up as she wrote, "Asking her out to dinner. Answered yes."

"Are they getting back together?" he wrote.

She didn't answer. Instead, she put her finger on the two buttons on the phone's base and gently pressed down. Then she silently settled the receiver back in its base.

"Does it matter?" she whispered. "They're talking. And that's all that really matters."

Chico leaned back into a big white faux-leather beanbag chair where his sister never let him sit. It made a swooshing sound as he nestled into the morphing beanbag shape. For a moment, her face scrunched up and he thought she was going to yell at him. But then the look faded and a gentler expression crossed her brow.

"Hey, I heard you'll be in honors math this fall. The principal called and told mother right after you left," Debra said as she reached out and messed up his hair. "Mother was so excited I thought she was going to have a spasm."

Chico looked up at his big sister who was now standing over him with a beaming smile on her face. "And I'm proud of you too, Chico. I believe Talula was right—it *is* time to drop the 'Boy.'"

Why was Debra being so nice to him? Was the world coming to an end? He didn't have to ponder the situation long because just about that time she picked up a neon blue flip-flop from the mess on her floor. Aiming it directly at his head, she threw it as she said, "Get off my beanbag, twerp!"

CHAPTER 15

Talula felt her eyes brim with tears. The moment was too beautiful. All of Miss Lancer's hard work had paid off—every detail from her crown of wild flowers to her simple white dress flowing in the breeze. She looked breathtaking. And Ben looked so handsome in his powder blue rented tux, his wounded arm in a matching sling. Talula closed her eyes and imagined Chico standing at the altar with her.

"Are you praying?" Big Mike whispered as he jabbed her side with his finger.

"Shh!" Chico whispered from the white folding chair on her other side.

"Sorry," Big Mike mouthed and turned his attention back to the ceremony.

Soon the preacher was telling Ben he could kiss the bride, and from somewhere behind them music began to play. This was Talula's cue to get ready to go inside the church fellowship hall to prepare to serve cake. Miss Lancer had given her specific instructions on how to do it. They'd even practiced together on a test cake. Suffice it to say, she didn't want to mess up her role in Miss Lancer's big day. Talula guessed she should call her Mrs. Lancer-Johnson now that she was married and she'd hyphenated her last name. "Lancer-Johnson," Talula smiled to herself. That sounded like some kind of weapon from a secret agent film.

Talula's revelry didn't last for long. Soon the happy couple were retreating back down the aisle and over to the small lake filled with swans. It was the perfect backdrop for photos. Very convenient of the church to have such a pretty lawn on its south side for weddings and family gatherings. She'd heard they made a fortune charging people a fee to use it. But then they turned over the proceeds to the town's food pantry. She guessed it all worked out for the good.

As Talula shot off towards the church fellowship hall to take her place as a server, she glanced back at Chico's parents. They had been sitting behind where she, Chico, and Big Mike had been positioned, up front, just behind the groom's family.

Debra and her latest boyfriend were sitting to the side of Chico's parents. At first she was surprised the family had attended together until Chico told her his sister had persuaded his mother that it would be best. He said Debra had reminded his mom of all Mrs. Lancer-Johnson had done for Chico as his school tutor. And, she reminded her that their father Sonny had been the one to introduce the happy couple a few years back. Debra also fudged the truth and said the bride herself had asked for them to attend the wedding together. It was all pretty much an outrageous lie on Debra's part. However, Talula noted, by the looks of it, Debra's fib seemed to be paying off because their parents were smiling and talking to each other.

Hurrying into the building, Talula stopped in her tracks and stared in amazement.

Wowza. Wowza. Wowza. The flowers. The decorations. Everything looked like a scene out of a bridal magazine. It was truly magical and utterly romantic all at the same time. In fact, it was making her heady. She could only dream her wedding reception would look this incredible.

Catching her breath, she looked across the way where a girl that was her serving partner motioned for her to come into the kitchen area. They needed to wash their hands and put on their server aprons before the guests started filtering into the reception. Talula rushed over to the kitchen and immediately moved to the sink where she found the soap. Carefully, she began sudsing her hands, taking extra precaution not to get water on her Sunday best dress.

As Talula washed, her server partner opened a big white box on the counter. With great care, she brought out matching fancy server aprons and handed one to Talula. The top apron strings had already been tied for them. Gingerly, both girls slipped the top part of the aprons over their heads. However, when they attempted to tie them in the back at their waists, they both were at a loss as to how to do it.

"Maybe we should tie each other's apron," the other girl suggested as she turned her back to Talula.

Talula's hands shook as she made a perfect bow, just as her mother had taught her several years ago. "There," she said as she finished. "You look perfect."

Now the question was if the other girl would be able to make her bow look as good. She guessed she would have to accept whatever bow she got as she couldn't see to do it herself. Forcing herself to take deep breaths, Talula calmed herself down. The girl trying her apron seemed to be doing a competent job as she pulled and twisted on the strings behind her, pulling it just snug enough to look good in the front without being uncomfortable.

"Oh, no. Here come the first guests," her serving partner said as she abruptly left Talula standing in the kitchen while she raced out to stand by their station. Soon the bride and groom would be coming in to cut the cake. Then they would begin to do their serving thing. It had been decided earlier Talula would cut the cake since she was the most skilled at it, and the other girl would serve the plates of cake to the guests.

A commotion of people talking excitedly outside signaled the bride and groom were headed their way. Talula looked over at her serving partner and smiled. It was obvious they both felt confident they were up to the task before them. Goodness knows, Mrs. Lancer-Johnson had made them practice enough. She was proud that Mrs.

Lancer-Johnson had selected and trained her. The other girl was a family member of Ben's so it was expected that she would be chosen, but Mrs. Lancer-Johnson selecting Talula had been an unexpected honor.

Chico and Big Mike came in the church auditorium door behind the bride and groom. His heart was a little sad that his first crush was a married woman now. But the fact that he and Talula were practically a couple eased the pain of his achy heart.

He watched as a red-headed woman took the bride's hand and led her over to look at a table laden down with gifts while another silver-haired woman pulled the groom toward the serving area where Talula and her server partner stood ready and waiting.

Chico neared the serving area so he could talk with Talula. Big Mike followed. As they approached, they heard the frazzled silver-haired woman say, "Ben, you need to go get her for the first dance and the cutting of the cake. There are a lot of people to serve and they're hungry."

Without a second's hesitation, Ben hurried over to his new wife who had her back to him.

Chico saw Ben reach out and lightly touch his hand to her shoulder in an effort to get her attention. Then, as if in a slow motion movie, the bride brought up both of her hands to her shoulder covering Ben's hand before rolling him over her back and flipping him in a martial arts maneuver that landed him in the floor lying face up on his back.

"What a smooth move!" Chico thought as the entire crowd stopped talking.

All of the wedding guests turned and stared at the couple in complete shock. Perhaps this was the reason no one rushed to help poor Ben, who was still lying face up, flat out on his back with a most surprised look on his face. Chico stared at the scene before him in disbelief. Behind him, he heard Talula say, "Good thing she didn't flip him by his wounded arm." Finally, his father Sonny came forward to help. The whole scenario only took a few moments from start to end, but it seemed much longer considering all that was involved.

The bride, now realizing what she had done, could only look down at Ben while she covered her mouth with her hands. It appeared she was going to cry.

Oh, no. Not before the first dance and cake cutting photos were taken.

But before she shed a single tear, Ben jumped back to his feet with a little assistance from Sonny and addressed the crowd. "Folks," he said with a beaming smile on his face, "I'm fine. Didn't even wrinkle my tux."

Then he took his bride in his arms and looked deeply in her eyes, "Dear," he said, "from this day forward, I promise never to sneak up on you again." Then he gave her a big kiss. You could hear a collective "awe" from the crowd that had formed around them.

When the couple drew apart, the bride was smiling and so was everyone else. Well, except for his mother and Sonny. They were just looking at each other—not in a mean way, but in a wary way. Chico noted they used to look at each other like this a few years back, before his dad left.

As everyone moved toward the center of the fellowship hall, Chico observed his father take his mother's hand and lead her toward a little room just off the main foyer. A lot of people used this room for prayer, but he doubted that was what they would be using it for. His heart lurched as he watched his mother reach up and wipe a tear from her cheek. They were fighting again.

The music stopped and the DJ handed over his microphone to Brother Lowe. A hush fell over the crowd as they waited. Brother Lowe tapped the microphone to check it before speaking, then he made the announcement they had all been waiting to hear. "To all the friends and family who have come to celebrate this marriage," he said with dramatic flair, "I would like to present for the first time ever, Mr. and Mrs. Johnson."

As the crowd clapped, the music came up and the newlyweds began their first dance. Chico knew they'd be cutting the cake right after this. Talula had told him this earlier as she explained the bride wanted to look fresh for the cake photos. And she didn't want anyone to miss out on the cake cutting ceremony. "There are a lot of older people at this wedding, and couples with babies," she'd said, "and Mrs. Lancer-Johnson didn't want to make them wait it out for the cake to be cut at the end of the wedding."

She also told Chico she admired Mrs. Lancer-Johnson for doing things her way on her wedding day.

"She's a strong personality and I'm determined to learn from her example."

Chico had been uncertain what to think about this comment as he loved Talula just the way she was. He also wasn't sure he wanted a girlfriend that could flip him like a flapjack on the dance floor. But maybe? Certainly he didn't want a 'fraidy cat for a girlfriend either.

The photographer was starting to take the wedding cake photos when Chico decided to sneak over and listen in on his parents' conversation. Approaching the small room from the left, he aligned himself on the wall outside. As the door was open, it would not be hard to listen in without being too obvious, and he needed to do it during the cake cutting photo session before the music and dancing started. The low roar of the crowd talking and laughing was enough of a problem already.

Moving as close to the door as he could without actually sticking his head inside, he stood perfectly still. His mother's tear-filled voice floated out around him. Not loud, but loud enough to show her anger and hurt.

"Sonny, what I'm saying is you've been trained to a point where you can't return to normal life. Jillian flipping Ben is further proof that it is instilled into the two of you to fight. Flipping Ben was second instinct to her, and Ben might've been hurt."

"No, Ben just surprised her and she rolled him on his back. He's not hurt. You saw him get up and brush himself off. If Jillian had wanted to hurt him, she . . ." Sonny's voice trailed off. Chico knew he was choosing his words carefully during the silence that followed because that was his father's way. He always thought before speaking and it'd served him well over the years. "Jillian loves Ben and she wants to make a home and family with him. That's why she's taken the teaching position here in town. It would be hard for her to be a mother and to have such a dangerous career path. And . . ."

His mother cut his father off. "Sonny, what's the difference? You are important to me and the kids, yet you choose danger."

"You know it's different being a mother."

"No, it's not. We need to know that you're not going to die when you go traipsing off doing your work. We need to know you won't get hurt." His mother's voice became choked as her tears flowed. "Let's be honest. You have a secret life, Sonny. One that you find much more exciting than the one you have with us. How can we compete with foreign locations? And secret missions? The kids and me . . . we've never been enough. And we'll never be . . ."

Sonny cut her short. "That's not true. That's not how I feel. You don't know how I feel. I miss you all so much when I'm gone. You guys are what keep me going. I love you all so much."

"Face it, Sonny. You're addicted to danger."

Chico looked up and saw a mirrored wall across the way. Not only did it reflect his eavesdropping self, it also showed his parents sitting across from each other in metal folding chairs. He considered moving to a more secure location, but then he reasoned his mother was watching Sonny, and Sonny had his head in his hands. So he stayed put and prayed that he'd blend like a chameleon that would go unnoticed if either of them looked in his direction.

Talula reached behind her to a small table that held a clean cup towel. Gingerly, she wiped the cake icing from her fingers before turning back to the big table that held the wedding cake and plates. She'd already gotten some of the icing on the expensive table cloth that had been so carefully selected for the occasion. And she felt bad about not being an expert cake cutter in spite of her training. Some of the pieces she'd prepared for her assistant server to hand out to people were less than perfect. In fact, some were a downright mess. But the guests didn't seem to mind. Everywhere she looked people were happily gobbling down cake and swigging punch. And those little mints that her server partner had set out in little crystal dishes were a big hit with this crowd. So Talula decided not to stress.

Besides, Mrs. Lancer-Johnson was too busy staring in her groom's eyes to notice the cake serving. Just as long as they got the job done, Talula felt like it would be okay. As she started to ease up on herself, she glanced across the room in Chico's direction. "What in the world was he doing pressed up against the paneled wall like that?" she thought to herself as he inched closer and closer to the open door on the wall. A most strained look was on his face.

Big Mike came up for another piece of cake. She

served it to him direct as her partner was out replenishing little mints.

"What do you think is up with Chico?" she said, casually gesturing toward their mutual friend. Big Mike turned and gave the situation his full attention before turning back to Talula.

"Hmmm," he said as he ate a piece of cake. "Chico's acting weird."

"Weird for Chico? Or just weird in general?"

"Weird in general," Big Mike said before continuing. "Look, he looks like he might cry. Do you think he's upset about Miss Lancer getting married? I know he has a crush on her, but I didn't think it was that bad." Talula's heart dropped to her gut and tears brimmed her eyes. Big Mike must have realized his mistake because he immediately started backtracking.

"But, of course, you and Chico are an item now, even though you're not officially old enough to date or go steady." His words tumbled out fast and hard as he continued, "I believe as Chico said when he gave you the necklace—you're promised to be promised and that's pretty serious. So I don't think he's at all upset about . . ."

As Big Mike stumbled on his last words, Talula watched Chico move away from the wall. Then, much to her astonishment, he started dancing near his sister Debra and her latest boyfriend. But he didn't look like he was having all that much fun because he kept glancing back at the open door. Then, he whispered something in his sister Debra's ear and she abruptly stopped dancing. Fire flashed in her eyes.

Both Talula and Big Mike watched openmouthed as Debra balled her hands up into two fists and headed full speed ahead toward the open door on the paneled wall. Chico was right behind her. And her boyfriend . . . well, he just continued dancing by himself.

Talula grabbed Big Mike's hand and said, "Let's go over and see what's up."

"Don't you have to serve cake?" Big Mike said between mouthfuls.

"Here, sit that down." Talula took his plate and fork from him and sat it on the edge of the serving table.

"Let's dance," she said as she pulled him over toward the open door and began furiously dancing.

"What dance are you doing?" Big Mike said as he tried to match her jerky moves.

"Shhh!" she said. "I'm trying to listen."

Suddenly Big Mike reached out and pulled her to him. Holding her tightly to his expansive chest, he lifted her off her feet and gracefully danced her over to the paneled wall. As he put her back on solid ground, he pointed up to an air vent just above her head. Cocking his head toward the metal vent, he motioned for her to do the same.

Their voices sounded hollow and far away inside the vent, but Talula could clearly make out Debra telling her mother to try and understand that she was asking for something that their father just wasn't equipped to give her. She wanted normalcy and he was far from normal. He'd never even come close to being normal. And, she reminded her mother, she would never really be happy with normal because she was not normal herself. That's why she loved their father in the first place. Talula considered Debra's convoluted reasoning and decided that she was pretty much on target.

Next, she heard Sonny's voice. It was lower and harder to understand through the vent, but she could hear the words "my father's house." He wanted his family to move to the neighboring town and live in his father's house that he'd inherited. In turn, he'd live in the trailer.

Sadness hit Talula like a speeding truck. It flattened her to think of Chico in a foreign town forty minutes away. They would never see each other as neither could drive for another couple of years.

But then Chico's mother started to speak. She didn't want to leave her job. She didn't want the kids in a new school district, especially when Chico was doing so well.

And that was all that Talula heard before the DJ announced it was time to toss the bouquet. In a blur, Debra rushed out of the prayer room and onto the dance floor where she positioned herself in a prime spot to catch it.

Talula and Big Mike casually moved away from the wall. Out of the corner of her eye, she saw Mrs. Lancer-Johnson preparing to toss the bouquet. But before she did, she turned and addressed all the females with a big smile. "Hold on a second, ladies. I have a great idea," she said. "I'll toss it from the half balcony upstairs. That will be more fair . . . and more fun."

Taking the steep stairs two at a time in her beautiful gown, Mrs. Lancer-Johnson was at the top in no time.

Seconds later, she appeared at the half wall overlooking the guests below. "Ready, girls?" she said as she turned her back and held the flowers up for all to see.

"Yes!" a dozen female voices squealed back as they jockeyed for position.

Talula felt Big Mike's hand on her shoulder giving her a little push forward. "Move up," he whispered. "You're too far away to catch it."

She hadn't even thought about catching it. Not until the actual moment when the bouquet was sailing in the air, way farther out from the half balcony than anyone had expected Mrs. Lancer-Johnson to be able to throw.

All the girls started backing up, trying to get what was just out of their reach. And Talula, who was already at the back of the pack, held up her hands in front of her face as the bouquet came flying straight at her head. *Kerplunk!* She felt the flowers against her cheek as her hands flew up to catch it. Her fingers grabbed lace and ribbon and she held on tight. The bouquet had come down so hard and fast her palms were red and stinging.

"Bullseye!" Mrs. Lancer-Johnson yelled down from the balcony above as she raised her fist in victory. "Can I throw a bouquet or what?"

Talula glanced over at the door on the paneled wall. To her surprise, Chico and his parents were standing outside, and all three smiling in her direction. She took this as a good sign.

Brother Lowe had asked Chico to meet him at the church

to go over the details of his baptism that was happening the next day. Never before had he thought of himself as a spiritual type person, but being baptized was pretty special. He didn't want to mess it up. In fact, he'd even brought Talula along to help him remember everything because sometimes when he was nervous instructions went in one of his ears and out the other.

While waiting outside the church doors, he saw Randall approaching in the parking lot. He knew Randall had also been saved at church camp, and Brother Lowe had already told him that he'd be getting dunked tomorrow, too. Who would have thought they'd be getting baptized on the same day?

As Randall approached, he pointed in Brother Lowe's direction and said, "What is that thing he's carrying?"

"Look, Chico!" Talula cried out. "Look what he's got!"

Turning, Chico couldn't believe his eyes. Brother Lowe was holding a couple of baptism gowns under his left arm. In his right hand, he carried a pogo stick—*his* pogo stick, the one that'd been stolen the day he and Talula were hiding inside the shed.

"Good morning," Brother Lowe said as he approached the trio. "I've got some things for you. Here guys, try on these gowns over your clothes to make sure they are long enough. You two are growing like weeds, so I had to guess at the size."

As Chico and Randall slipped their gowns on over their clothes, he noticed Randall was indeed taller than he'd been a month ago at camp. He suspected he was, too. "Boy, what a difference a summer made," Chico thought to himself. Brother Lowe inspected the length of the gowns. "Perfect fit," he announced.

Not one to be patient. Chico could wait no longer as he pointed at the pogo stick.

"Is that mine?"

"I believe so," Brother Lowe said as he handed it to him. "Arnold Simpson asked me to make sure I got it back to you. Said it was important."

"I can't believe he gave it back," Talula said as Chico took the pogo stick from the pastor.

"Arnold's not a bad man," Brother Lowe said. "He just made some bad choices."

Chico put both feet on the stick and started to bounce. *Boing, boing, boing.* He bounced across the church parking lot with his flowing baptism gown flying behind him.

"Hey, Chico! You kind of look like the nun that flies around on that television show." Randall called out. Both Talula and Brother Lowe laughed out loud. Chico heard, but he didn't care.

His spirits soared higher with each bounce. It was hard to feel anything but joy zooming through the air on this beautiful August day. Sure, everything in his life wasn't perfect, and he had a feeling they never would be perfect. But right now, he felt good. And that was enough.

MORE BOOKS BY
GINA HOOTEN POPP

The Storm After
(Winds of Change Series – Book 1)

Lucky's Way
(Winds of Change Series – Book 2)

The Emigrant's Song
(Winds of Change Series – Novella)

Tomorrow Comes At Midnight

67598664R00126

Made in the USA
Charleston, SC
16 February 2017